SAVAGE INTERLUDE

James St Just was Kate's half-brother, but for family reasons they wanted the fact kept secret—with the result that Damien Savage had jumped to all the wrong conclusions about Kate. And as in a very short time he had become the only man in the world for her, she had quite a problem facing her . . .

SAVAGE INTERLUDE

BY
CAROLE MORTIMER

MILLS & BOON LIMITED
17–19 FOLEY STREET
LONDON W1A 1DR

First published 1979
Australian copyright 1979
Philippine copyright 1979
This edition 1979

© Carole Mortimer 1979

ISBN 0 263 73155 3

Set in Linotype Plantin 10 on 11 pt.

*Made and printed in Great Britain by
Richard Clay (The Chaucer Press), Ltd., Bungay, Suffolk*

For
J.

CHAPTER ONE

'YOU had no right to do it, James. No right at all!' Kate smoothed back her almost waist-length hair, now pulled back and secured on the top of her head, the gold flecks in her brown eyes more vivid in her anger. 'Why must you always interfere?' she demanded.

James looked up from the script he had been casually perusing, a faint smile to his cynical lips. 'I had every right, Kate. Humphries is not for you.' He threw the script down on the sofa beside him.

Tears filled her eyes. 'No one will be for me if you carry on like this. As fast as I become interested in someone you effectively get rid of him.' She sat down dejectedly in the chair, throwing one bare leg over the arm.

He snorted with laughter, getting up to refill his glass with a liberal amount of whisky. 'You're only eighteen, Kate dear. Stop trying to latch on to the first man you meet. You have plenty of time to meet the man of your dreams,' his lip turned back in a sneer, 'you don't have to rush it.'

Kate pouted sulkily. 'But I really liked Nigel. He could be fun.'

James shrugged. 'Can't they all? And take that sulky look off your face. Damien Savage will be here soon, and with you glowering at him like that he isn't likely to stay long.'

'Good,' she returned childishly. 'Who wants to meet Damien Savage anyway?'

'I do,' he told her dryly. 'This film script isn't bad.'

'Up to your standard, brother dear?' she taunted.

He frowned his displeasure at her flippancy. 'I'll stop you

7

seeing Susan if you don't stop picking up her mannerisms,' he warned darkly. 'And don't call me brother, you know I don't like to advertise the fact that we're related.'

'Neither did your father,' she put in shortly.

'*Our* father,' he corrected.

'Mm, that was a closely guarded secret until he died.'

'Stop grouching,' he grinned. 'He made provision for you in his will, didn't he?'

'Oh, yes. And dragged me from obscurity into a life of gaiety. Like hell he did!' she added fiercely. 'He forced you to accept me into your life, took me away from the people I knew, and now half the people we know think I'm little more than your——'

'Calm down, Kate! My—our—father was a much respected man in the business world, and I'm not exactly unknown myself. And there's my mother to think of. What do you think it would do to her if it came out that her husband had fathered you?'

'It wouldn't help your reputation much either,' she grimaced. 'So in the meantime everyone thinks I'm your mistress, woman, whatever.'

'And they think I'm a cradle-snatcher. What the hell, I couldn't give a damn about what people think. It does me no harm to be thought to have my mistress in residence, none at all. And this way I can protect and look after you as our father intended.'

'So I've noticed. For the past two years, since I insisted on leaving that dreadful boarding school you sent me to, I haven't been able to do anything, see anyone without your say-so. It's so restricting!'

'Now come on, Kate. You aren't exactly deprived of meeting people. Look at the crowd we have this weekend.'

'All of them your friends,' she flashed back at him. 'The distinguished, the famous, the handsome, the *notorious* James St Just. You've appeared in so many films that have been shown all over the world that we can't go anywhere or do anything together without you being recognised.'

'You knew that when you demanded to be taken away from school.'

'Yes, but I didn't ask to come and live with you instead. I thought the school was bad, but this place is like a prison in comparison!'

'Don't exaggerate. You have everything you could wish for here—clothes, money, friends. You want for nothing.'

'Except love.'

He laughed at her woebegone face. 'I love you, funnyface. What more can you want?'

'Indeed,' drawled a voice behind them, the faint American accent only slightly noticeable. 'It would appear that Miss Darwood has what numerous women in the world would gladly give up everything else for.'

'What the hell——!' James sprang to his feet, turning to face the intruder. 'No one is allowed in this part of the house—Damien! By all that's holy! But I told Jennings to show you out to the pool when you arrived.'

Green eyes narrowed. 'I didn't come all this way to be fobbed off to the pool with your other guests. I'm sorry I interrupted your tête-à-tête with Miss Darwood, but I have a limited time in England, and all of it accounted for.'

The voice was attractive enough, deep and faintly husky, but what he was saying wasn't. And the contempt in those deep green eyes wasn't very pleasant either. Kate had seen numerous photographs of this famous man, but no photograph could do him justice. It couldn't begin to hint at his height, well over six feet, or the blackness of his hair, and the deep emerald of his eyes. His face was deeply tanned as if he enjoyed being out in the sun, his features harsh, from the thinned contemptuous lips, the taut aquiline nose, to the deep lines grooved either side of that satanic face.

'Come in, come in,' James invited, unperturbed by this

man's terseness. 'Of course you don't have to go to the pool if you don't want to. Can I offer you a drink?'

'Whisky will be fine,' Damien Savage nodded consent.

James poured out the whisky for his guest himself. 'I've read the script, Damien. I like it.'

The film director looked at Kate pointedly. 'Could we discuss this somewhere more private? The script is not for the public yet.'

'Kate isn't the public,' James laughed. 'I have no secrets from her, you can talk quite freely.'

'Nevertheless I would prefer that we spoke alone.'

James shrugged. 'Would you mind, Kate?'

She looked from her brother to the arrogant face of Damien Savage. 'But I——'

'Please, Kate.' Her brother's eyes were pleading.

She glared at Damien Savage. Damn his arrogant face! He walked in here looking like the devil himself, dressed completely in black from head to foot, and proceeded to order everyone about. Well, she would do as James asked this time, but if that man dared to order her about again, she would ...

'All right,' she agreed ungraciously. 'I'll see you later, James.' She deliberately ignored Damien Savage, but from the bland look on his face that didn't bother him in the slightest.

She swayed gracefully out of the room, well aware that her perfect figure was shown to advantage in the pale green bikini she wore. What an arrogant devil that Damien Savage was! His importance as one of the leading film directors in the world must have gone to his head. Goodness knows James was famous enough in his own right, but even he had seemed rather overawed by the man's dominating personality.

'Kate darling,' Sheri greeted with her low American drawl. 'Where's James?'

Kate sat down next to the tall junoesque Sheri, admiring

the other girl's cool blonde beauty. Her own red hair often led to her losing the fiery temper that went with that hair, no matter how she tried to prevent it happening. She had been having another heated argument with James only minutes earlier, about his ruling concerning her friends. In fact, it hadn't yet been settled, Damien Savage had seen to that. Damn the man! With James in his rare good humour of the last few days she could perhaps have managed to make him change his mind about Nigel. Who knew what his mood would be like the next time she saw him?

'He's inside,' she told Sheri. 'With Damien Savage.'

'Damien's arrived?' Sheri's blue eyes lit up excitedly.

Kate grimaced. 'Oh, he's arrived all right. Sweeping all before him.'

Sheri gave a husky laugh. 'That sounds like Damien. He doesn't suffer fools gladly.'

'Are you saying I'm a fool?' Kate demanded indignantly.

'Oh dear, has he upset you already?'

'You say that as if he does it often.' Kate looked at the other girl interestedly. She had only ever seen newspaper reports about Damien Savage's women friends and what a brilliant director he was, nothing about the rest of his life. But there had been plenty about the women in his life; he always seemed to be involved with one leading lady or another.

'He's very—blunt,' Sheri told her.

'You've met him before?' she couldn't help her interest.

'Mm,' Sheri sipped her lime juice, 'at a couple of James' parties in London. He's very good-looking, and so masterful.'

'I can think of a few other choice words to describe him. I don't like him at all. And James surprised me, he more or less let him walk in and take over.'

'You do that with Damien. And to appear in one of his movies is to guarantee success, and you know how James loves success. Damien never fails. I think it's all to do with the fact that he writes them as well as directing them. He's brilliant, everyone accepts that.'

'Oh, I admit he's clever, I've never denied that. But does he have to be so bossy with it. I didn't——'

'James!' Sheri stood up to greet him, pursing her lips to receive his kiss. She hugged his arm to her side. 'Kate was just telling me you'd been delayed. Damien, how nice to see you again,' she smiled at him.

'Sheri,' he nodded curtly, those piercing green eyes now hidden behind dark glasses.

'I didn't realise you'd be coming here today,' she said conversationally.

His look was scathing. 'At least James didn't feel it necessary to inform *all* his guests of my plans.'

Kate knew he was referring to her and she felt her hackles rise. He had a nerve! Why shouldn't James discuss things with her? She might only have been in his care four years, but during that time they had become as close as any normal brother and sister who had been brought up together.

James was twenty years her senior, and a very famous film star into the bargain, but he always had time for her—sometimes too much time, which was when they had their arguments. But he had been very good to her since he had learnt on his father's death that he was not an only child after all, but had a fourteen-year-old-sister by another woman. Kate had been in an orphanage since her mother had died and it had seemed like a dream come true to suddenly find that her brother was James St Just, and that he intended looking after her.

She had every reason to feel grateful to him, and so on being allowed to leave school at sixteen had set out to become his friend and confidant. And she had succeeded, although there were still certain things he shut her out of, times when he could be stricter than a father, and these were the times she wished he didn't take his guardianship of her so seriously.

She rejoined the conversation at Sheri's suggestion that they go for a swim. 'Not you, Kate,' James said sternly. 'You've only just eaten your lunch.'

'Oh, but——'

'You'll have to excuse me too, I'm afraid,' drawled that infuriating voice. 'I've just eaten myself.'

'Oh!' For a moment James looked undecided. 'Oh well, we can talk again later. Just ask one of the staff for a drink and relax for a while.'

He and Sheri ran to the pool's edge before diving into the clear blue water, leaving Kate alone with the man she already heartily disliked. Too magnetically attractive and arrogant for his own good, that was her opinion. She made a move to leave. 'Well, if you'll excuse me ...'

She was stopped from leaving by the firm, blood-stopping grip of his hand on her wrist. She looked down at that hand, even in her discomfort admitting that it was a nice hand, strong and sensitive at one go, and not at all rough as she had imagined it to be.

He smiled mockingly as he interpreted her surprised glance. 'Surely you aren't going to leave me alone, Miss Darwood—Kate? I'm sure James wouldn't like you to do that.'

She was sure he wouldn't either. Bother the man, he was too damned sure of his own importance! She subsided back on to the lounger, watching him from behind her dark glasses as he slid on to the one next to her. 'Are you working on a film at the moment, Mr Savage?' She had learnt during the last couple of years that there was nothing most of James' friends liked more than talking about themselves.

'Damien, please,' he said smoothly. 'Yes, I'm working on a film at the moment. Do you enjoy this sort of life?' She was startled by the suddenness of the question, expecting the next fifteen minutes or so to be spent in boredom as she pretended to listen to him praising himself. 'Lounging about poolsides,' he continued, 'and no doubt attending numerous parties.'

Kate had to admit she had attended a few, but only with James in close attendance. She shrugged. 'It's okay.'

'Okay!' he snorted his disgust. 'Wasting your life away here! Why don't you get yourself a job instead of hanging around here like some sort of expensive groupie for St Just and his rich friends? Go out and meet life head-on instead of sitting here waiting for it to come to you.'

Kate had visibly stiffened at his use of the word groupie, and had gone on to burning anger. She sat up rigidly. 'You don't have the faintest idea what you're talking about, Mr Savage, so I'll try to ignore all your insults.'

'I don't want you to ignore them, I want you to listen and take note. You have good bone structure, good colouring, in fact you're quite beautiful. Have you ever had a screen test?' he shot the question at her.

'No, I haven't. James wouldn't like it.'

He gave a cruel smile. 'I can imagine. Probably because with the right tuition you could be a bigger star than he is.'

'And I suppose you think you're the person to give me that tuition,' she said sarcastically.

'I could be,' he replied deeply.

'I thought so. You're just another wolf, Mr Savage.' And she had met plenty of them the last couple of years.

To her surprise he smiled. 'At least I don't dress up in sheep's clothing. I meant what I said about you becoming a bigger star than James. Come round to the studio on Monday and we'll see about that screen test.'

'With the contract finalised on the couch in your office, no doubt?' she returned.

'Oh no,' he smiled. 'We're a little bit more sophisticated than that nowadays. I take you back to my apartment for the night,' that taunting mouth mocked her. 'Can you act, by the way? It isn't really necessary, but it would be a bonus if you can. Of course you can act,' he answered his own question impatiently. 'You're doing it here all the time.'

'I am not! I don't like you and I'm making no pretence about it.'

'I don't ask that you like me, just that you turn up on Monday. And why should you pretend to like me when James openly admits to loving you? He's rich enough to keep you in luxury for the rest of your life—or until some-one richer comes along. Just as a point of interest, *I* am richer than James.'

'So?' she asked insolently.

He shrugged. 'I just thought I'd save you the trouble of having to find out my bank balance.'

'As I'm not interested in *you* your bank balance doesn't interest me either,' she told him angrily. The conceit of the man!

He was watching Sheri and James' antics in the pool. 'I suppose you're used to sharing him with other women. James doesn't seem to be able to settle down with just one woman.' He was looking at her behind those dark glasses and she wished she could see the expression in his eyes. 'You've lasted quite a long time now, a couple of years at least. Although it doesn't seem to have stopped his other little diversions. How old are you?' again the question was shot at her so suddenly it took her by surprise.

'Eighteen,' she answered jerkily. 'Nearly nineteen.'

He nodded his dark head, his hair over-long and brushed back in the casual windswept style that was fashionable at the moment. 'That's what I thought. And you've been living with St Just since you were sixteen,' it was a state-ment, not a question. 'Don't your parents mind? Or don't they care what you do?'

'My parents are both dead.' Poor Mummy, who had to live with the guilt of having borne an illegitimate child, and her stepfather who had never let either of them forget that they owed their respectability to him. Given the same circumstances herself, Kate would have preferred to have remained unmarried rather than put up with Arthur's abuse day and night.

Her mother and stepfather had been killed in a road accident when she was only fourteen and as she had no other family she had been put into care. Unbeknown to her she did have other family; her real father had been made aware of her existence from some papers left for him by her mother. Unfortunately the knowledge of his daughter's existence had brought on a heart attack, closely followed a couple of months later by another one, this time fatal. But in his will he had left her to the guardianship of his only son, James St Just.

'Perhaps that's as well,' that hateful man interrupted her thoughts. 'I don't think they'd like to see what you've become.'

'I haven't *become* anything,' she told him angrily. 'I've done nothing to be ashamed of.'

'Nothing?' He raised one dark eyebrow. 'So that's how you've managed to keep St Just interested. I should warn you, I don't play by the same rules.'

'I can imagine. You don't appear to be a gentleman.'

Her comment caused him some humour, and she watched in fascination as his mouth curved into a smile, showing even white teeth. 'No,' he agreed, 'I think we can safely agree that I'm not a gentleman. That's why I find it quite easy to invite you to a party with me this evening.'

'This evening? But James is expecting you to stay here overnight.'

'Then he's going to be disappointed. I'm in England for three days only and then I return to Hollywood. I have a lot of things to do, a lot of people to see.'

'And I'm not one of them,' Kate said firmly, hoping to make her escape.

'You're an unexpected bonus. And I mean to take advantage of it.'

'But not of me,' she told him vehemently.

'That could be arranged. I'll be leaving in about an hour's time, be ready to go with me. Bring something with you to wear to the party, you can change at my apartment.'

'No, I can't, because I'm not even leaving the house with you, let alone going to your apartment.' How dare he suggest such a thing to her!

He stood up in one lithe movement. 'I wouldn't be too sure of that. I should talk to James first before you say a definite no, he wants this part in my film pretty badly. The party tonight is being held by Matt Strange, he wants that part too.'

'But I—— That's—blackmail!' she glared at him.

'All I did was invite you to a party. Be at the front of the house in an hour, I don't want to have to come looking for you.' He left her to join a group of people on the other side of the pool, instantly becoming the centre of attention.

James touched her shoulder with one wet hand. 'Why so deep in thought?' He picked up a towel and began to dry his bronzed body. 'Have you fallen for our enigmatic director too?'

'No, I haven't. I think he's awful. Conceited and arrogant! He had the nerve to order me to go to a party with him tonight—I say ordered because he certainly didn't give me any choice in the matter.'

'Tonight?' James frowned. 'He isn't staying here?'

'I would have thought that was obvious when he's invited me to a party.'

'All right, Kate,' he sighed. 'Just calm down. The man's a damned nuisance. I expected to get him slightly inebriated, introduce him to a couple of nice girls, and then get his agreement to my playing the lead in his next film.'

Kate looked at him closely. 'I thought the part was already yours?'

James slipped on a knitted blue top. 'Matt Strange is after it too. But I want this part, Kate, I want it badly.'

'I thought you said the script wasn't bad. That doesn't sound like the part of a lifetime to me.'

'All an act, Kate. The part is brilliant. And I'd be good in it, I know I would. And I need this part, Damien never fails.'

'I gathered that,' she said dryly.

He grinned. 'You're in the minority as far as women go, they usually go down like ninepins. So where is he taking you?'

Kate's eyes widened. 'He isn't taking me anywhere. I told him I wasn't going.'

He bit his lip. 'I wish you hadn't done that.'

'You can't be serious, James. I don't want to go to Matt Strange's party. I don't like him any more than I do Damien Savage,' and she looked at him anxiously.

'Look, Kate, I'm at the top of my profession now, as far as I can go without starring in a Damien Savage film. Most of his films are for an unlimited budget, he can do what he damn well pleases. And no matter what he does it's always a smash hit. Anything new he tries and all the other film companies take it up too. I'm not getting any younger, and there won't be too many more opportunities for me to play a part like this one.'

'Thirty-eight isn't old,' she put in disgustedly.

'It is to still be playing the hero. There's too much young competition appearing on the scene, Matt Strange is only twenty-seven. Pretty soon I'll start having character roles offered to me. Oh, I won't mind, at least I'll still be working. But they aren't leading roles.'

She couldn't miss the look of pleading in his eyes. She had never thought of his career in this light before, he always seemed to have so much money and be constantly surrounded by other television and film stars. The money could be easily explained, the St Justs had their own family fortune, and the so-called friends would fade away as fame did.

'But he wants me to go to his apartment with him first,' she told him desperately, seeing her chances of getting out of this becoming slimmer and slimmer. She loved her half-brother, and if her going to a party with the hated Damien Savage was going to help him in any way, then she would go, no matter what her own feelings were in the matter.

James pursed his lips thoughtfully. 'That can easily be got around,' he said carelessly. 'You can go to our apartment and meet him later.'

'But I don't like the man!' Her plea was only half-hearted now, as she realised that James was really serious about her going out with Damien Savage. She wished she didn't feel quite so much as if she were selling herself to further her brother's career.

He smiled. 'You're only going to a party with him, you don't have to like him for that.'

She raised her eyebrows. 'And how does the evening usually end for you and your date on these occasions?' She saw his face flush knowingly. 'Exactly,' she told him dryly.

'He won't expect that of you on your first date. He won't expect that of you at all, I won't allow it!'

Kate had to laugh at his determined expression. 'You can't very well stop it a hundred miles away.' All humour left her face. 'But I think I should warn you that even though I may love you and want to help you, I am not prepared to go to bed with the arrogant Mr Savage to do it.'

'You haven't been asked yet,' came the dry comment from behind them. 'And there's every chance you never will be.'

Kate blushingly turned to face Damien Savage, wondering just how much of the conversation he had heard, and what construction he had put on it. 'This seems to be becoming a habit,' she said shortly.

'That's right,' he agreed unconcernedly. 'And now that

you've both declared your love for each other perhaps you would like to get some things together. I plan to be on my way in about fifteen minutes.'

Kate looked appealingly at James. 'I—I haven't said I'll go with you.'

He looked at her brother too, arrogance in every line of his superb body. 'Do you have any objections to my taking your—to my taking Miss Darwood to a party this evening?'

James evaded Kate's pleading eyes. 'Not if she wants to go.'

'I——'

'She does,' Damien Savage interrupted coolly. 'I'll return her to you some time tomorrow. I'll also let you know about the part.'

That was a veiled threat if ever she had heard one, a threat that meant she had no choice but to go to her room and get the requested clothes. She did so with ill-grace, slamming about her bedroom throwing clothes uncaringly into the open suitcase on her bed. Why should she have to go out with someone she disliked? More to the point, why did he want to go out with her?

Well, if he thought he was going to have an affair with her he was going to be disappointed. She didn't go in for that sort of thing. But he wasn't to know that! To all intents and purposes she was living here quite openly with James, without thought of marriage. So how was Damien Savage to know she wouldn't be just as willing to have an equally intimate relationship with him? Because she would tell him, that's how he would know!

James and Damien Savage were still at the poolside when she came out a few minutes later. She walked up to James' side, leaning intimately against him. She saw the other man's mouth tighten disapprovingly and smiled more warmly at her brother. What Damien Savage didn't know couldn't hurt him, and she had no intention of telling him of her family tie to James.

'Are you ready to leave now?' he asked shortly.

Kate looked at him coolly. 'My case is in the hallway.' She had changed into slim-fitting brown trousers and a matching shirt, leaving her hair smoothed back on top of her head. Her mother had always refused to have the flaming red hair shorn, and although it could be a nuisance at times she too kept it to its long length.

'We'll be on our way, then.' He picked up his discarded jacket.

She looked quickly at her brother. 'James, the apartment,' she reminded him pointedly.

Damien Savage looked at the two of them impatiently. 'What's wrong now?'

James looked uncomfortable. 'Kate would like you to drop her off at our apartment in town so that she can change.'

'I've already said she can do that at my apartment.'

'Yes, well——' James laughed nervously. 'She would rather go to ours, and it isn't that far from your own. You could drop her off and then pick her up on the way back.'

Damien sighed heavily. 'If that's what the lady wants.'

She *wanted* to stay here, but he was making that impossible. 'I do,' she told him firmly.

'Right.' Damien put out his hand to James, giving the proffered hand a firm shake. 'Thanks for the hospitality, James. See you tomorrow some time.'

'Yes—right. Fine. Well, have a nice time this evening.' James looked at Kate anxiously, trying to find some sign of softening towards him in her rigidly held features, and finding none. 'Kate?'

She stood on tiptoe to kiss his cheek. 'Goodbye, James.' There was no warmth for him in her voice either.

'Come on,' Damien Savage said impatiently. 'I don't have time to waste.'

'So you've already said,' she returned tartly.

He frowned his displeasure at her tone before marching through the house and out to his car parked on the fore-court. He didn't wait to see if Kate followed him, but she knew he expected it, and with a resigned shrug in James' direction she did so. The car was as impressive as the man, a black Lotus Elan. She knew the make of car because James had thought of buying one last year before finally settling for a Ferrari.

After stowing her small case in the back of the car he climbed in beside her, settling back comfortably in the low seat. 'I thought we were never going to get away!'

Kate answered less sharply than she would have done normally, all too much aware of how close they were in the compact interior of the car. 'Why did you come in the first place if you felt that way?'

'I had to see James. Besides,' he added tauntingly, 'I may not have met you if I hadn't.'

'And I'm sure you would have been devastated.' She admired the way he handled the car, going fast but always in complete control of the vehicle, not a movement wasted.

He gave a grin and she was amazed at how much less forbidding it made him, and younger, much younger. But then he couldn't be all that old, mid thirties at most. 'I doubt I would have been devastated, a little disappointed, maybe, but nothing so extreme as devastation. I've seen you before, of course.'

Her brown eyes widened. 'You have?'

'Mm,' he looked thoughtful, his strong tanned hands manoeuvring the car without need for concentration, al-most as if the vehicle were a part of the man himself. 'Usually on the news, getting on or off a plane with James,' he continued. 'It's amazing we've never met before.'

Kate looked uninterestedly out of the window. 'Amazing isn't quite the word I would use.'

'I should think lucky fits in more with your idea of things.' He glanced sideways at her. 'James must want this part pretty badly to allow me to walk off with his girl.'

'I'm not his girl!' she snapped.

'You're hardly more than that. Eighteen years of age!' he said with disgust.

'Nearly nineteen,' she put in resentfully.

'How nearly nineteen?'

'Well, I—In eight months' time!'

'Like I said, eighteen years of age. And already you have someone like James St Just in love with you. You have me intrigued too, if that's any consolation to you.'

'It isn't,' she said firmly.

'Look, kid, the James St Justs of this world will only use you. You'd be better off with people of your own age, people who don't want you for what they can get.'

She glared at him angrily. 'Is that why I've been forced to come with you?'

'I didn't force you. If there was any forcing done it was by James. I merely requested that you come with me.'

'Requested!' she scoffed. 'You blackmailed me.'

His green eyes narrowed. 'And how did I do that?'

'You—you threatened me.'

'I did no such thing,' he denied mildly.

'Well, you threatened James, then,' she blustered. 'You more or less said that if I didn't accompany you to this party you'd give the part to Matt Strange, the part James wants.'

'My dear girl——'

'I'm not your *dear* anything,' she interrupted.

'My dear girl,' he continued as though she hadn't rudely interrupted him, 'if I intended giving Matt Strange that part then believe me he'd get it, no matter what bribe James put in front of me. Even if you are the most beautiful thing I've seen in years.'

'Then you don't intend giving Matt Strange the part?'

He shook his head. 'No, James is definitely right for it, he knows it and I know it.'

'Then why——'

'Why the supposed indecision?' he finished for her. 'I never believe in letting my actors become too sure of themselves, and a little healthy competition does them no harm at all.'

'So you've already decided to give James the part?' she demanded, a feeling of indignation beginning to well up inside her.

Damien Savage nodded. 'That's right.'

'So I have no need to be here really?' Her fiery temper was definitely beginning to take over now.

The look in his eyes could only be described as intimate. 'I wouldn't say that.'

'Well, I would!' Kate turned fully in her seat to glare at him. 'You have a damned nerve! You're like a puppeteer, you pull the strings and everyone moves as you tell them to. I don't like you, Mr Savage, I don't like you at all.'

'I know,' he admitted calmly. 'I think that's half your attraction to me.'

'I don't want you to find me attractive. I——' She suddenly noticed that he had pulled the car to a halt. She looked about her dazedly. This was an apartment block, but it certainly wasn't where she and James had their apartment. 'Where are we?'

He was already getting out of the car. 'At my apartment.' He came round to open the door for her.

'But I—— You said you'd drop me off at James'!' she accused.

'So I did,' he taunted. 'But you didn't honestly believe I would, did you? Let's go,' he continued. 'I promise not to look while you change.'

CHAPTER TWO

KATE hung back, glaring at him indignantly. 'I know you won't look while I change, because I'm not changing anywhere near you. I'm not going anywhere near your apartment either. I'm not completely naïve!'

Damien Savage looked down his haughty nose at her. 'And I'm not going to suddenly leap on you as soon as the door is closed behind us. I have more finesse than that.'

'I can imagine,' Kate returned dryly.

'I'm sure you can, little girls like you often have vivid imaginations. Don't be such a coward, Kate!' he snapped. 'What harm can it do you to come up with me, take a shower, change, and then go on to a party?'

Put like that it sounded quite innocent, but how could she be sure it would be with a man of his reputation? 'I—I'm not sure,' she looked at him uncertainly.

Damien was no longer looking at her but had turned his attention to the man who had left the apartment building at their arrival. 'Good evening, Barry,' he greeted the man, handing over his car keys. 'I'll be needing it again about eight-thirty.'

'Right, Mr Savage,' the younger man smiled.

Damien Savage raised a taunting eyebrow at Kate as she still sat inside the car. 'Ready?' he asked softly.

He left her no choice but to follow him, which she did with ill grace. She fumed silently all the way up in the lift, hardly aware of her surroundings, except to note absently that they were plush and obviously the height of luxury. She would still have liked to refuse to come up here with this man but had baulked at causing a scene in front of the other man. As he had known she would!

25

The lift doors opened directly into the penthouse apartment and Damien Savage stepped out into the luxurious interior, waiting only fleetingly for Kate to follow him. He led the way silently into the lounge, moving forward to switch on the stereo before turning to face her.

The music that pervaded the room was soothingly melodious and not jarringly obvious as most music seemed to be nowadays. In fact the whole room was decorated for comfort and not for fashion, and it instantly found favour in Kate's eyes. A three-piece suite in deep brown leather stood before the mock fireplace, a deep-pile cream carpet adding to the warmth and relaxation of the room, an antique mahogany dresser and stereo unit completed the furnishings.

Damien Savage was watching the play of emotions across her expressive face. 'I take it my home meets with your approval?'

'It's—it's very nice,' she replied awkwardly.

'But not what you expected,' he guessed shrewdly.

'Hardly.'

'You'll have to go to James and his friends if you want the ultra-modern decor they seem to find attractive. Personally, I think it's hideous and totally unrelaxing.'

'So do I.'

'You agree?' he looked surprised.

'Certainly. You didn't expect that, did you?'

'No,' he answered honestly. 'But I like women who can surprise me.'

The faintly intimate tone to his words reminded her of her reasons for being here. 'Your likes and dislikes in women don't interest me,' she said sharply. 'Nothing about you interests me.'

'I'll do my best to change that,' he promised deeply, his green eyes caressing.

Her lips turned back in a sneer. 'I shouldn't bother. I

doubt my opinion of you will alter with better acquaintance.'

'You never know,' he taunted. 'I've been told that I can be quite charming on occasion.'

'I won't ask what occasion,' she said bitchily.

He chuckled at the disapproval in her face. 'Perhaps you're right. Would you like me to show you your room?'

'My room——! You can show me where I'll be changing,' she corrected. 'But it certainly won't be my room.'

'I'm not going to argue with you—yet. I'll take you to *the* room now. I only have someone come in to keep the place free of dust and stock up the refrigerator, I manage everything else on my own,' he continued conversationally, taking her down a short corridor and into a bedroom on the left-hand side. 'I'm not in one place long enough to keep permanent staff.'

Kate could well believe it; he always seemed to be reported to be moving to one location or another. She liked the bedroom, the huge four-poster bed, the Queen Anne furniture. What extraordinarily good taste this man had, quite surprisingly so.

'This is lovely,' she told him appreciatively.

'Changed your mind about staying?'

'No! Definitely not.'

He shrugged. 'I'll leave you to sort out your clothing while I fix us something to eat.'

She couldn't imagine the worldly, sophisticated Damien Savage doing that and she protested loudly. 'I'm not hungry,' she lied.

'Rubbish. I'm pretty good at cooking omelettes, light and fluffy as they should be,' he added temptingly. 'And I can have it ready in about five minutes.'

She ignored the rumblings of her stomach. 'Why should you want to get me a meal?'

Damien Savage sighed. 'I happen to be hungry myself. It's quite some time since I last ate.'

'Oh well.' Kate turned away to begin taking out her gown for the evening. 'In that case I might as well join you. I'd love an omelette.'

'With salad?'

'With salad,' she agreed.

She didn't need to turn to know he had left the room, she just sensed it. This was the strangest day she had spent since the day she had suddenly been introduced to James' unusual but interesting life. Strange, because a few hours ago she hadn't even met Damien Savage; she had had the usual girlhood dreams about him a few years ago, but now she was actually in the bedroom of his apartment. Her immature daydreams had never taken her this far.

She hung up her dress on a hanger she found in the closet. It was a black silk gown, so it hadn't creased too much in the case. An hour or so on a hanger should ensure that it had no creases at all.

Dinner was ready for her when she came into the kitchen a few minutes later. A place was set for her at the breakfast bar and she sat down without a word. Damien sat next to her and they ate in silence.

He heaved a sigh of satisfaction as he drank the last of his coffee. 'Right,' he stood up. 'I'll go and shower and leave you to clear this away.'

'You'll what?' Kate looked at him in amazement, pushing back a stray wisp of hair that had escaped her topknot.

'You heard me. I'm not going to wait on you all evening.' He stopped at the door. 'And wear your hair loose tonight,' he ordered.

'I will not!' She faced him, a slender defiant figure in her fitted trousers and blouse. 'I hardly ever leave my hair free.'

'For me you will,' he promised softly. 'I love long-haired women. How long is it?'

'Almost down to my waist,' she told him sulkily. 'And I don't want to be classed with your women!'

'I don't have any women at the moment,' he answered

with some amusement. 'Only a little girl that I'm finding more desirable every moment I'm with her. I like females that answer me back,' he surprised her with this disclosure, 'and you do little else.'

'If I'd realised that I would have been so nice to you you would have longed to get away.' The golden flecks were more noticeable in her wide brown eyes. 'I wish I'd known!'

'Too late,' he laughed huskily.

Left alone in the kitchen, Kate had little choice but to wash the dishes and tidy them away. By the time she had finished Damien was back, dressed only in a black silk robe that reached just above his knees, his strong tanned legs bare beneath its short length, and the V-neckline showing her the thick dark hair that grew on his brown chest. He had obviously shaved, and droplets of water still glistened in his hair where he had showered.

He watched her over the flame of his lighter as he lit the long cheroot in his mouth, smoke drifting about the room. 'Your turn,' he said softly, his green cat-like eyes never leaving her face.

She was disconcerted by his complete unselfconsciousness at his almost nakedness, her nostrils appreciating the aroma of the cheroot. 'I—er—couldn't you have dressed before coming back in here?' she demanded defensively.

He shrugged his broad shoulders. 'Why should I? I live here.'

'Yes, but—but *I'm* here.'

'So? I'm wearing more now than James was this afternoon, and yet you didn't appear shocked then.'

'That was different, and you know it,' Kate accused. 'Now we're alone, and you—well, you aren't dressed.'

Damien gave a half smile. 'Come on, honey, I'm quite adequately clothed, and you're just wasting time. It's seven-thirty already.'

'All right, I'll shower and change. And for goodness' sake get dressed!'

The smoke wafted about his head. 'I intend to—in my own good time.'

Kate moved to the door, but he blocked her exit. Her eyes were riveted to the dark hairs on his chest and she couldn't raise her eyes any higher, fearing the mockery in his eyes. 'Will you let me pass, please?' Her voice was a husky whisper and she cursed herself for her timidity. But he was so overpowering, so essentially *male*.

He moved slightly aside, but not far enough for her to pass through without touching him, and she didn't want to do that. 'Go ahead,' he encouraged, smiling tauntingly.

Kate set her lips determinedly and brushed past him, her body coming into full contact with the hard muscle of his. She recoiled away from him instinctively, hating herself for her weakness. She walked hurriedly to the room Damien had given her to use, closing the door firmly behind her.

God, how he unnerved her! Much as she hated to admit it, it was an inescapable fact. She had met men like him before, arrogant, darkly attractive, but none of them had ever affected her as he did. She was constantly aware of him, mainly in anger, but sometimes as a vibrant attractive man who demanded attention unconsciously.

And he *was* attractive, much more handsome than most of the men who appeared in his films. He could almost have been a film star himself, in fact he had been at one time, until directing had interested him more. And he was good at his job, excellent in fact.

But he frightened her; she wasn't up to the sophisticated games he seemed to be constantly engaged in. She didn't need two guesses as to his interest in her, but under James' guardianship she wasn't even allowed to date the same man more than a few times, let alone indulge in promiscuous affairs. But she felt sure Damien Savage didn't plan a platonic friendship between the two of them, it wasn't his way at all.

What would she do if he tried anything like that on her? What *could* she do? She certainly wouldn't give in to him. She couldn't do that, although she was sure he could be very persuasive.

A warm shower and fresh make-up and she felt more confident of herself, and once she had on the figure-hugging black dress she felt a hundred per cent better. It was a strapless dress, finishing abruptly as it rested on her firm uptilted breasts, smoothing down over her narrow waist and slender hips. It suited her and she felt good in it.

Damien was in the lounge when she came out of the bedroom, looking handsome and sophisticated in black trousers accompanied by a blue velvet dinner jacket, the startling white shirt he wore opened casually at the neck. His eyes slowly travelled up her body, pausing momentarily on her breasts with a probing insolence, finally passing on to her face. She saw him frown in the subdued lighting of the room. 'Your hair,' he snapped, his eyes narrowed. 'You didn't listen to what I said earlier.'

'I did.' She held herself stiffly. 'I just didn't want to do it.'

'Do it now,' he commanded.

'No,' she shook her head.

'Do it, Kate, or I'll do it myself.' He made a threatening step towards her. 'And I probably won't be as gentle as you would.'

She put up a self-conscious hand to her confined hair. 'It looks a mess when it's loose,' she said uncertainly, put off by the determined glint in his eyes.

'I mean it, Kate.'

'But—but we'll be late! It's already eight-thirty, the car will be downstairs.'

'It can wait, and so can the party for that matter.' He stood firm, and she knew by the arrogant lift of his head that he wasn't going to relent.

She threw down her evening bag angrily on to a chair, beginning to pull out the pins that secured her hair. 'Oh, all right! But don't blame me if you feel like drowning me halfway through the evening. This hair of mine seems to have a life of its own when it isn't confined.' She ran her hand through the long loose waves of her red hair, tumbling it down her back like a shimmering flame.

Damien's eyes never left her. 'Beautiful!' he breathed softly. 'I'm even more convinced that you'll be photogenic.'

Kate was brushing her hair in long vigorous strokes, feeling it crackle with healthy life. 'I'm not going to that screen test, you know,' she tugged viciously at a tangle.

'Why not? Frightened I meant it about coming back to my apartment for the night?' he mocked her.

'Not at all,' she answered with a confidence she didn't feel. 'I'm just not interested in what people call stardom.'

He raised a surprised eyebrow. 'You're not?'

Kate shook her head, her hair now a silken curtain of fire down her back, the red and gold lights in it brought into more prominence by the black of her gown. 'Definitely not.'

Damien moved forward with a triumphant laugh. 'I think I'm really going to like you, Kate Darwood. The most beautiful hair I've ever laid eyes on and no bid for stardom! You sound like perfection to me,' he bent his dark head with a suddenness that took her by surprise, catching her off guard as he claimed her lips possessively with his own.

For one mesmerised moment Kate let him kiss her, even allowed herself to respond for a few short seconds, before good sense took over. She was here alone with this man in his apartment, completely at his mercy if he should choose to take advantage of the situation.

She fought against him, wrenching herself out of his arms. 'Stop that! What do you think I am!'

'I already told you that.' He watched her with amusement, glancing at his wrist watch. 'You're very beautiful. And we're going to be very late if we don't leave now.'

'I've been ready for the last ten minutes,' she said crossly.

He handed her her bag. 'And I'm ready to leave now.'

Kate sat bolt upright on her side of the car, the soft music from the cassette doing little to soothe her nerves. How dare he kiss her like that, as if he had a perfect right to do so? James had much to answer for, letting this man calmly walk off with her as if she were an *object*, and she would tell him so when she got back home. When she got back . . .

'Are you annoyed because I kissed you?' He gave her a sideways glance.

'You had no right to do it,' she obstinately refused to look at him, even though his eyes compelled her to.

'I had the right of a man attracted to a beautiful girl,' he told her haughtily. 'Or do you save all your kisses for the faithless James?'

'I don't save any of them for him.'

'Perhaps that's as well. He's very keen on Sheri, you know.'

Kate did know. At first she had felt a sisterly jealousy towards the American girl, her own new-found relationship with James still so fresh that she felt a certain possessiveness towards him. But she had found that his obviously growing affection for the other girl made no difference to his loving care regarding herself, and so instead of being a hated enemy Sheri had become the female confidante she badly needed.

'I do know,' she said tightly.

'And it doesn't bother you?'

'Why should it? I'm not his keeper. He's a grown man, old enough to choose his own friends.' She hoped they were nearly at Matt Strange's, at least among the crowd that were likely to be there he wouldn't be able to keep taunting her in this arrogant way of his.

'As long as he comes back to you you don't particularly care.'

'Now look, Mr Savage, I don't particularly *care* for your accusations, and if I could I would put you right about a few things. Unfortunately it's not up to me.'

Damien had turned the car off the main road, down a short narrow lane, and into a long gravel driveway. The mansion at the end of the driveway was bathed in bright lights, and there seemed to be people in every room as Kate looked in at the uncurtained windows. There were obviously curtains there to be drawn, but as the evening was so warm the windows and doors stood wide open. The noise coming from the building was tremendous, and from the amount of cars parked in the large driveway she would say there were hundreds of people here, just what she needed to avoid this man.

He parked the car behind another one equally expensive and sleek. 'Don't tell me,' he mocked. 'You're secretly married to James.'

'Something like that,' she nodded.

'Which means you *aren't* married, which also means I don't give a damn about St Just and the hold he has over you——'

'There *is* no hold over me!' she cut in.

'Which means,' he continued as if she hadn't spoken, 'I intend to have you for myself.'

'Wh-what do you mean?' Her eyes widened.

'You can't be that innocent. I've made no secret of the fact that I want you. St Just knew it, that's why you're here with me now, and you know it too, don't you?' His look was caressing.

'And do you get everything you want?' The question came out huskily; she was affected by the look in spite of herself.

'Usually.' One strong hand caressed her creamy cheek, touching and parting her soft lips. 'Am I going to get you?'

'No,' she answered firmly, hoping she sounded more convincing than she felt. She found it hard to articulate at all, that hand causing strange sensations in her inexperienced body. What had James done, allowing her out with this—this rake! This man emitted sex-appeal without any conscious effort on his part, the heat of his body and the smouldering look in his green eyes enough to turn her legs to jelly.

He moved slightly, bringing his body up close against hers, their two heartbeats sounding as one. 'Are you sure about that?' His breath ruffled the hair at her temple, the smell of his aftershave and the cheroots he smoked invading her nostrils to make her aware only of him.

Kate felt mesmerised by the sleepy passion she could see in his eyes, dragging her own gaze away with effort. 'I—I think so,' she answered breathlessly.

Damien gave her one last lingering look before he straightened, opening his car door to come round to her side of the car and help her out of the low vehicle. 'Then you're going to be wrong,' he promised softly against her ear, towering above her in the evening's fading light.

'I am?' she squeaked.

'You are.' He took her elbow to guide her through the open front door of the mansion and into what seemed to be a lot of raised voices, chinking of glasses, and very loud music.

Everywhere Kate looked there were people, most of them known to her vaguely from James' parties. The laughter and chatter was overpowering and she felt sure that most of the people here were halfway to being drunk already.

'Damien!' They both turned at the sound of that husky voice. Diana Hall, the star of a popular television series, came over to greet him. 'Damien, I've been waiting for you to call me,' she pouted. 'You said you would.' Her short black curls bounced provocatively around her ears, her mouth was painted a vivid scarlet.

Damien raised one dark eyebrow. 'I did?'

She giggled. 'You know you did, the last time we were together. I remember we were——'

'Diana, do you know Kate Darwood?' he interrupted her, frowning darkly.

Blue eyes focused on Kate, darkening with recognition. 'Is James here this evening?'

Kate knew that this was a spiteful dig on the other girl's part, and she knew by the scowl on Damien Savage's face that the dig had gone home. 'No,' she replied softly.

Those narrowed blue eyes turned on Damien. 'Have you been doing a little kidnapping of your own, Damien?' she taunted. 'I always thought you despised James' association with a girl young enough to be his daughter.'

The glitter in those green eyes was the only sign that he was at all angered by the last remark. 'I'm hardly old enough to be Kate's father,' he returned smoothly. 'Her uncle perhaps, but as that isn't the way I think of her I don't think it applies.'

Diana bit her bottom lip, the bright smile she gave in the next few seconds not quite reaching her narrowed blue eyes. She looked at Kate. 'Do I take it that James is now a free agent again? Or are you going to hold on to two of the world's most eligible men?'

Kate could see by the brightness of her eyes that the other girl had had too much to drink, otherwise she might have lost her temper at her rudeness. As it was she thought Diana Hall would have much to regret in the morning; Damien wasn't someone she herself would like to anger, and he was certainly angry.

'I've never even held one, let alone two,' she replied evenly.

'Excuse us, Diana,' Damien cut in abruptly. 'We haven't said hello to Matt yet.'

'He's outside somewhere. I can take you if——'

'That won't be necessary,' he said curtly. 'We can find our own way.'

Still guiding Kate by the elbow, he led her through two more rooms equally crowded with people and out on to the patio. It was much cooler out here after the oppression of the smoke inside and Kate heaved a sigh of relief at not being jostled about any more.

Damien lit a cheroot. 'I'm sorry about that,' he said shortly. 'Diana isn't usually so bitchy.'

Kate leant against the wall overlooking the garden, the illumination out here almost as bright as inside. 'That's all right. But I think you should just warn me in case any of your other girl-friends decides to throw a tantrum about my being here with you. The next one might get violent.'

He gave a reluctant smile, his harsh features softening at her sarcasm. 'She was that obvious?'

'As one of your girl-friends?' She saw him nod. 'Very obvious. Do all your women get as possessive about you as she has?' she asked tauntingly.

'Apparently not, by your attitude towards me.'

She blushed. 'I'm not one of your women.'

'Yet,' he added softly.

'I thought you despised men who chase young girls.' He couldn't mistake the contempt in her voice.

Amazingly he wasn't angered by her taunt, but laughed softly. 'I'm thirty-three years of age, that makes me fifteen years older than you, and it doesn't bother me in the slightest. All it means is that I have the experience to match your youth.'

'Experience in bed, you mean!' she snapped.

He nodded. 'If you like. Does my age bother you?'

'Why should it? I've already told you, I'm not interested in you, sexually or otherwise.'

'We'll see.' He seemed to lose interest in the subject, much to her chagrin; she would have liked to insult him some more. 'Actually, talking to Diana gave me an idea. This thing between James and you—is he your father? Is that the link between the two of you?' he pinpointed her with his eyes.

Close, but not close enough. 'No,' she told him calmly, 'James isn't my father.'

'Mm,' he was broodingly thoughtful. 'There's some mystery here. Looking at the two of you together I would swear you've never belonged to James. Would I be right?'

'Why should I tell you that?'

'Why not?' He wasn't looking at her but searching the garden with narrowed eyes. He turned to face her, his eyes holding her immovable. 'Your virginity doesn't interest me,' he said dryly. 'I merely wondered how intimate your relationship with James had been.'

Kate's mouth twisted at the casualness of his tone. Damien seemed to find it easy to talk of such things, and although she lived in the midst of the permissive society, James protected her from any situation that could become in the least intimate. But he wasn't here now, she was in this on her own! 'I don't really think that's any of your business,' she told him stiffly.

His lean body so close to her was rather unnerving—and she thought him well aware of the fact. 'Oh, I think it is,' he returned mildly. 'I want to know what limit of competition I have.'

'Competition!' she repeated scathingly. 'With your conceit I'm surprised you allow for such things.'

Damien quirked an eyebrow at her. 'You think me conceited?'

'I don't think it at all—I know it. Dragging me off whether I wanted to come with you or not appears to me to be the height of conceit.' She gave him a disgusted look.

'But I already knew you had no intention of coming with me unless I made it impossible for you to refuse. Your affection for James gave me the leverage I needed.' His eyes taunted her. 'The first and only time I've ever used my supposed privileged position. Let me assure you, I'm not in the habit of using blackmail to get what I want,' he shrugged. 'In your case I'm afraid shortage of time made it impossible for me to do anything else.'

'What do you mean?'

'I have tomorrow and part of Monday left in England, then I return to my home in the States. That doesn't give me a lot of time to get to know you.'

Kate would have liked to have informed him that she had got to know him as well as she wanted to, but thought better of it. No doubt he would have given her an equally blistering reply. There didn't seem to be much that would ruffle this cool self-assurance of his, and she felt certain she wouldn't be able to do it.

'Does it matter?' she asked casually.

'That I get to know you?' His eyes deepened with an emotion she didn't care to analyse but thought she recognised as desire, blatant unhidden desire. 'Oh, I think so, don't you?'

'Not at all.'

'Oh, Kate,' he shook his head, a slight smile to his lips. 'I'm not that frightening, am I?' He stilled the nervous movement of her hands, gently lifting one to kiss her palm. 'Am I?' he watched her keenly.

She tried to pull her hand away, but his hold tightened, making it impossible for her to escape his grip. Her clenched hands had been a purely unconscious movement and she resented him for seeing it. 'You're not frightening at all,' she said crossly. 'Not at all.'

He was prevented from answering her by the appearance of their host, a tall blond-haired, blue-eyed man, very handsome in a rugged sort of way, accompanied by a girl on each arm. He had never been popular with Kate and she couldn't hide her disgust at the two giggling girls gazing up at him adoringly. But then he was always surrounded by girls.

'Damien,' he shook hands with the other man. 'Diana told me you were here somewhere.'

Damien gave an easy smile. 'You're not an easy man to find. Kate and I came out here to get out of the crush.'

Matt smiled. 'Invite a couple of people over and the whole world turns up.' He turned those light blue eyes on Kate, eyes that she hated, horrible leering eyes that undressed her with one look. 'And I see you have the beautiful Kate with you. Did James come too?'

'No,' Damien snapped. 'Kate and I came alone.'

'Oh, I see.' Matt looked surprised. 'I naturally assumed ...'

'Well, don't,' the other man replied shortly. 'Just accept that she's here with me.' He looked disapproving. 'This sort of atmosphere isn't really suitable for what I wanted to say to you.'

'By your choice of partner I would say I already know what you have to say.'

Damien frowned deeply. 'Kate being with me has nothing to do with our conversation. Do you have somewhere more private we can talk?'

Matt looked down at the two girls at his side. 'Get lost, girls,' he laughed at their pouting looks. 'I'll find you both again later, I haven't forgotten your promises. But it must be business before pleasure. We'll go to my study, Damien.'

Damien looked at her with those startling green eyes. 'Kate?' he caught her attention. 'Will you be all right here for a few minutes?'

She looked hurriedly away from Matt Strange's taunting face, not particularly wanting to be left alone here but not wanting to say so in the face of such mockery. 'I'll be fine. Why shouldn't I be?'

He nodded distantly. 'Indeed.'

Kate was regretting her obstinacy several minutes later, standing on the edge of the crowd, knowing she didn't fit in here. She usually managed to avoid parties of this kind, only occasionally attending one with James. She had never realised quite how nervous she felt about these people, all of them drinking and smoking too much. She had even had a couple of drinks herself in an effort not to look quite so much like an outsider, and she was beginning to wish she hadn't now; the alcohol had gone straight to her head.

'Kate!'

She blinked rapidly to clear the smoke from her eyes. 'Nigel!' her eyes lit up with pleasure. 'How nice to see you.' He would never know how much! She had just about been ready to run, feeling totally out of it standing here.

He looked around nervously, an often shy, fast-speaking individual who had become quite a good friend the last few weeks, she had hoped perhaps more than a friend. Until her brother had interfered! 'Is James here?' He had obviously been thinking along the same lines as herself.

She laughed naturally, suddenly feeling more relaxed. 'Anyone would think we were a double act. You're the third person to ask that this evening.'

'Well, let's face it, you hardly ever go anywhere without him,' he laughed shortly. 'So how did you get here?'

Kate was just about to answer him when she felt an arm slide about her waist and pull her close against another human being, distinctly muscular and male. 'She came with me,' Damien Savage answered for her.

She watched Nigel's instant recognition, resenting the way he smiled ingratiatingly at the other man. And she had thought herself almost in love with him—how could she, when he didn't even seem to mind that possessive arm about her waist! Well, she minded, she minded very much.

'Mr Savage,' Nigel gushed. 'How nice to meet you.'

'Likewise,' drawled the older man, his American accent more noticeable. 'Are you ready to leave, honey?'

She watched Nigel's face for any reaction to Damien's implied intimacy between them—and found none. Obviously her growing affection for this man had not been returned. 'Ready,' she answered in a soft pliant voice, her anger towards Nigel making her feel more friendly towards Damien.

'Do you have to go?' Nigel looked disappointed. 'I've wanted to meet you for so long, Mr Savage, and it's——'

'I'm ready, Damien,' she said firmly.

'Okay, Kate. Some other time.' He smiled coolly at Nigel before taking Kate's hand and leading her out of the house. He turned to her in the confines of the car. 'Who was that?' He accelerated out of the driveway.

'Nigel Humphries,' she answered shortly.

'A friend of yours?'

'I believed so.'

'But not any more?'

'I don't think so.' Not if he couldn't feel normal jealousy. 'He's an actor,' she supplied, suddenly realising just what a good one he was. He had really had her thinking his interest was solely in her, but she knew now she had just been a way of getting to James.

'I've seen him in a couple of small roles. I didn't like you talking to him, Kate. I didn't like it at all.'

Kate was too busy panicking to answer him. He had driven past James' apartment yet again. He was taking her to his home!

CHAPTER THREE

But of course he was; they had to pick up her case yet. Kate felt herself relax again, cursing herself for her stupidity. She shouldn't suspect all his motives like this, she was getting a positive complex about the man. She must get herself out of this near-hysterical state, laugh a little, act more naturally. As he had said earlier, he wasn't suddenly going to leap on her. She was just being silly, blowing everything up out of proportion because of his reputation.

Back in his apartment again she wasn't so sure. He seemed in no hurry to leave again, offering her a drink and helping himself to a whisky at her refusal. She had already downed the two Martini and lemonades during his ten-minute absence at the party, finding herself drinking them quickly because she was nervous, out of her depth without James at her side. Consequently the rapidity of the drinks had made her feel slightly merry; another drink would probably push her over the borderline between merry and just plain drunk. Alcohol had never been one of her strong points, and already Damien Savage didn't look quite such an ogre to her. He looked handsome and exciting—most of all exciting.

'Was Matt Strange annoyed about not being given the part?' she asked steadily. Oh goodness, it must have been the night air that had made her feel like this; two drinks didn't normally make her feel so—so much like laughing and singing at the same time. She made an effort to look serious, feeling a humorous twitch to her lips. Whatever was the matter with her!

'No.' Damien moved to turn out the main lights, leaving the room illuminated by just three side-lamps. It was de-

43

finitely more cosy this way— and more dangerous. Kate felt her trepidation grow as he came to sit beside her on the sofa, his thigh only inches away from her own.

She licked her lips. 'He—he wasn't?'

'Nope.' He moved closer, their thighs almost touching now, his arm across her shoulders. He had discarded the velvet jacket and unbuttoned several of the top buttons of his shirt in the heat of the apartment.

Kate shifted uneasily under the sensuous look in his mesmerising eyes. 'Er—why wasn't he?' Goodness, he was close, and she did feel so strangely lightheaded.

'One simple reason.' His voice had lowered seductively. Damien wound one long strand of her hair about his fingers, making it impossible for her to move. Not that she wanted to, she was quite enjoying being this close to him, feeling his warm breath softly caressing her cheek.

'Why was that?' She licked her lips again, fascinated by the deep cleft in his chin.

'I offered him the other leading role,' he gave an amused smile.

That pierced her fogged-up brain. 'The—the *other* leading role?'

'Mm.' He bent his head to caress her throat slowly with firm passionate lips. 'There are two male leads.'

Those lips were causing strange fluttering sensations in her body, but it was a pleasant feeling, one she didn't want to stop. This was Damien Savage, the man she had fantasised about at the great age of thirteen, before her devotion had passed on to someone she had believed to be more attractive. She had been wrong; no one could be more attractive than Damien, or more sexually exciting.

But at thirteen she hadn't known of such things, and as she grew older she had felt her devotion turn to embarrassed dislike, her mind accepting that it was ridiculous to fantasise about men she was never likely to meet, and with the arrogance of youth she had dismissed him from her mind. But now she *had* met him, only to find her fantasies more than coming true.

He was kissing her as she had once imagined he would, but it wasn't at all like she thought it would be. It was more, so very, very much more. It was exciting and frightening at the same time, his lips a very pleasurable sensation on her bare shoulders.

'Damien, I——' She fought for control of her senses; she mustn't let who he was colour her judgment. But it wasn't who he was that was affecting her, but what he was doing to her. 'Damien, please!'

He raised his head slightly. 'Yes?' His eyes were half-closed with emotion. He ran a hand through the hair at the side of her face, and gentle caressing fingers down her flushed cheeks. 'Such wide innocent brown eyes. They promise so much and yet withhold much more.'

'A-about the film,' she forced herself to sanity. 'James won't be very happy about working with Matt Strange.' She pushed back her tousled hair and sat up straight on the sofa, making an effort to move him further away from her.

Damien scowled, not relinquishing his hold on her. 'I couldn't give a damn about James' happiness. He either works with Matt or he doesn't do the movie at all, the choice is his. But I should think the fact that I intend taking you away from him would bother him more than working with Matt Strange.'

'But you can't—I mean, why should you——'

His lips returned to the softness of her perfumed throat. 'Because I'm going to take you away from him any way I can. You're going to come and live with me, Kate.'

She moved against those probing lips, his tongue licking flames along the sensitive cord in her neck. 'I'm not, you know,' her words were fevered, her mind fogging once again. 'My home is with James. He takes care of me.'

'I'll take care of you,' he promised huskily, his mouth

travelling slowly towards her waiting lips. 'Much better care of you than James ever could.'

'No, no . . .' Her protests didn't sound very firm and she knew Damien was aware of it, felt rather than saw his smile of triumph. That should have been her moment to stop him, the moment she should have stopped that mocking, arrogant mouth taking possession of hers.

But she didn't, she allowed his firm mouth to part and claim her own, gave herself up to the pleasure he evoked. She had been kissed before, she wasn't completely innocent, but she had never been kissed in quite this way before. His lips teased and deepened the kiss, teased and deepened it until she moaned against him, her body moving to meet his, begging for more than he was giving.

When the onslaught finally came she wasn't prepared for it, her body relaxed from his hands upon her fevered skin. Suddenly she wasn't sitting any more but stretched out lengthwise on the sofa, Damien's long lean length close against her. Her hands were up around his shoulders, touching his warm skin inside his now fully unbuttoned shirt. Her eyes were closed, her throat bared to the warmth of his lips.

'Oh, Damien,' she breathed, knowing she would regret this later but for the moment not giving a damn. 'You go to my head,' she admitted softly.

His green eyes smouldered down at her. 'I don't think I'm solely to blame for that. How much have you had to drink?'

She touched that fascinating dimple in his chin, something she had felt tempted to do ever since she had seen him for the first time yesterday. 'I only had two,' she answered vaguely.

'At Matt's?' he asked sharply.

Kate pouted up at him, admiring his lean tough body in the close-fitting shirt and trousers. 'Mm,' her tongue slowly moistened her lips. 'Is it important?'

He groaned in his throat, burying his face in her hair. 'Not right at this moment. God, you're lovely!' He looked down at her. 'I wish you wouldn't do that.' His eyes were tortured.

She looked up at him innocently. 'Do what, Damien?'

'Lick your lips like that.' His mouth briefly covered hers. 'It's very provocative.'

'She smiled happily. 'Is it?'

He smiled too. 'You've definitely had too much to drink. And I'm not sure I'm up to this sudden change. A little while ago you would have fought like a she-cat not to be in my arms.'

Her look was one of pure challenge. 'What's the matter, aren't you interested now that I'm no longer fighting you? Are you one of these men who enjoy the chase but not the capture?'

'You silly child, I want you, whether you fight me or not. I must say I prefer you soft and pliant in my arms, but if it has to be a fight then a fight it will be. Victory can be very sweet.'

'You're sure you'll win then?'

'Oh, undoubtedly,' he confirmed softly.

Kate laughed slightly. 'You're very arrogant, Damien. A veritable devil, in fact.'

'Mm, are you complaining?'

'I——' her voice faltered, her head began to swim. 'I feel strange, Damien.' Her voice sounded faint to her ears. What on earth was wrong with her?

He raised his head to look down at her suddenly pale face. 'Oh no,' he swore angrily, shaking her roughly. 'Those drinks, what were they?' He sat up, looking down at her anxiously.

Her mind didn't seem to be functioning. She ran a hand over her aching temple. 'I—er—I can't remember.' Her eyes were wide with distress.

His grip tightened on her forearms. 'Come on, Kate, think. Answer me!'

'I—It—Martini and lemonade—I think,' she added lamely, starting to feel sick now.

'Oh, hell!' His mouth tightened. 'And was Jerry Saunders in charge of the bar? A stocky man with long dark hair and wearing glasses,' he explained at her puzzled look.

'I—I think so.' Her eyes just wouldn't focus, Damien's features were taking on a hazy shape that didn't seem to make sense.

'God, I could kill him! The stupid——! Just wait until I see him again, I'm likely to do him some physical damage.'

'I don't understand, Damien. I—I want to go home. I feel ill.'

'But you aren't going home, especially not in this state.' His hand smoothed back her hair. 'You're staying here tonight, with me.'

She shook her head. 'No—no, I have to go home. I mustn't stay here, Damien, I mustn't.' She swung her legs to the ground, attempting to stand up and falling back down again. 'Damien, I think I'm going to . . .' she collapsed back against the silk cushions in a dead faint.

Damien shook her, but to no avail, his face contorted with rage. 'Damn and blast Jerry to hell!' He picked her up and carried her to the bedroom.

Kate awoke with a feeling of well-being, the bedclothes pulled right up to her chin. She moved her head slowly, not quite sure where she was. Then it all came back to her—Matt Strange's party, coming back to Damien's apartment. She even vaguely remembered what had taken place on the sofa. And then nothing.

Her face flushed a fiery red. What had happened after that? What had she done? More to the point, where was she? This bedroom didn't look familiar, in fact it wasn't even the one with the fourposter bed that Damien had shown her into yesterday. No, this was a much more masculine looking room, the decor in subdued green and cream. It was a man's room. It had to be Damien Savage's bedroom!

But what was she doing in here—— That was a stupid question! It must be obvious to anyone what she was doing in here, what must have taken place in this very room the night before. Oh God, no! Surely he hadn't—— But what other explanation was there? If only she could remember, if only everything hadn't seemed in such a haze.

She sat up, forcing herself to think calmly and not to panic. It wasn't easy, especially as her sitting up revealed that she seemed to be wearing a black silk pyjama jacket, a man's pyjama jacket that was much too big for her. It reached almost down to her knees as she stepped out of bed, obviously meant for a much larger person than herself. Damien...?

'Good morning, angel,' he drawled, walking into the bedroom, a cup of coffee in one hand and some buttered toast on a plate in the other. And he was wearing the pyjama trousers that belonged to the jacket she had on! Nothing else, just the trousers. 'Your breakfast,' he smiled at her.

Kate looked away, ashamed of her instantaneous response to his bare muscled chest, her breath suddenly feeling constricted in her throat. 'I don't want it,' she mumbled.

He tilted up her chin, smiling with taunting humour. 'What's the matter, Kate? You weren't sulky like this last night.'

'Last night!' she hissed. 'You tricked me, let me get drunk so that I couldn't think straight, and then you——' she broke off in embarrassment.

Damien quirked a mocking eyebrow. 'Then I what?'

'I don't know what you did next,' she said impatiently,

glaring at him accusingly, 'but I'm sure you didn't just put me to bed in *your* room and then meekly sleep somewhere else.'

'You're right,' he nodded. She followed his gaze to the rumpled bed, her eyes taking in the twin indentations in the pillows placed side by side. 'We both slept in that bed,' he confirmed.

'Oh no!' She put up a hand to her flushed cheeks, unable even to look at him.

'Oh yes,' he told her lightly. 'And you can blame Jerry Saunders for getting you drunk. Your Martini and lemonades were liberally laced with vodka. It's a famous party trick of Jerry's. You went out like a light.'

'Then you——' she looked confused. 'You didn't——'

'No, I didn't,' Damien answered shortly. 'I'm not in the habit of making love to unconscious women.'

Her confusion deepened. 'But you—— I *was* in your bed, and you did say you slept there too.'

'That's right, and slept is the right word. You're really quite affectionate when you're asleep. You snuggled up to me like a baby.' He smiled, as if the memory of it pleased him.

It didn't please Kate one little bit, she still wanted to know what had or had not happened the night before. She looked down at the pyjama jacket. 'This,' she pulled at the pocket. 'How did I get into this?'

'How do you think?' He laughed at her shocked face. 'Don't worry, honey, you aren't the first female I've undressed and taken to my bed. Although they haven't usually passed out on me,' he added in that mocking voice she hated, his glittering green eyes openly laughing at her.

'But did you have to put me in this?' Her anger was all the stronger at the thought of him removing her clothes.

His smile deepened. 'Would you rather I'd left you naked? I must say that the idea did appeal to me, but even I have a limit to my control. As it is you've nearly driven me insane with wanting you, squirming about in my arms all night. It was only the trusting smile on your face that held me back.'

'Couldn't you have put me in my own nightclothes?' She remembered the sheer baby-doll pyjamas she had packed and blushed at the picture that conjured into her mind.

'Quite,' he grinned as he read her thoughts, then picked up a piece of her toast and walked to the door. 'Believe me, you were safer in that. Wait for me here—I'm just going to shave. You see how thoughtful I am, I wouldn't like to scratch your delectable skin with my night's stubble.' He ran a rueful hand over his darkened skin.

'Scratch my skin?' she repeated dazedly.

'Mm, when I come back and make love to you.'

'You—you aren't going to do that!' She backed away from him, angry with herself for revealing her fear of him.

He halted his exit, the burning passion in his brooding eyes belying her words. 'I'm not?' he asked softly.

Kate clutched the pyjama jacket to her, cursing its inadequacy. She must look perfectly ridiculous, verbally denying him and yet here in *his* bedroom, wearing *his* clothing. The very air between them was full of intimacy, making a mockery of her and her denials. 'No, you're not,' she said crossly. 'As soon as you get out of here I'm getting dressed and leaving as soon as I possibly can.'

'You are?'

'I am,' she told him firmly.

Slowly he reclosed the door, his lean body as taut as a bow. 'Then you'll just have to suffer the stubble on my chin. I'm not giving you the chance to walk out on me. You cheated on me last night, I'm not giving you the opportunity to do it again.'

All the time he was moving closer to her, the black silk pyjama trousers resting on the arrogant swagger of his hips. She seemed to be mesmerised by the male beauty of him, the completely male aura he emitted, an aura as dangerous to women as a jungle cat to its prey. The only trouble was that Damien had his sights set on something much more prized than food.

'I—I didn't cheat,' she denied desperately. 'I had no intention of going to bed with you, either now or last night.'

He was standing so close to her now their thighs almost touched. His hard strong fingers moved up to part and caress her lips. 'Such a kissable mouth.' His eyes were half-closed with feeling. 'And you've already been to bed with me, the only difference this time will be that I intend taking what you've clearly been offering all night. The only reason I haven't already taken advantage of your offer is that I happen to like my women sober and responsive when I make love to them. And last night you weren't either of those things.'

'You aren't going to make love to me! I—I don't want you to.'

'That wasn't what you were saying to me last night before you passed out,' he murmured caressingly, his slight nudge to her shoulder knocking her off balance so that she fell backwards on to the rumpled sheets. He lay down beside her, his legs pinning her to the bed. 'Your lips were telling quite another story then. Let's see if it's still the same one.'

Her protests were swallowed up by the savagery of his mouth on hers, by the way his hands took possession of her body, moulding her to him until she could feel the hardness of him against her. She knew that she shouldn't respond, but her body seemed to have a will of its own as she pressed against him, her arms clasped firmly about his neck as she played with the hair at his nape.

He bent to kiss each closed eyelid, moving her hands to his firm muscled back, groaning his pleasure at her caresses. He nibbled her ear-lobe, one hand inside the open neckline of the jacket she wore. She tensed as his hand travelled down to cup her breast, the nipple rising tautly to his touch. She made a half-hearted movement to stop him, but his hand remained adamantly in place, his fingers firmly clasping her soft smooth skin.

Kate felt herself lost in a wonderment of strange new feelings. She felt wonderfully relaxed in his arms, a complete freedom of inhibition, and yet there was also a searing sense of tension rising swiftly within her, feelings that threatened to overflow and explode when she wasn't ready for them.

He slowly slid down her body, his lips raining fevered kisses wherever they touched, his fingers swiftly tackling the restrictive buttons to push aside the silky material and expose the taut flesh beneath. His eyes turned almost black in colour at the naked sight of her.

'God, you're beautiful,' he groaned. 'Like a marble sculpture—but with much more warmth.' He cupped her naked breast, smoothing the soft firm flesh. 'You'll never know the effort it cost me not to take you a hundred times during the night,' he told her huskily, kissing each breast hungrily. 'A hundred, a thousand times!' he moaned his torment.

'Oh, Damien . . .' she quivered her uncertainty. 'I——'

'No,' he put a gentle hand over her mouth. 'Don't talk, honey. Just let go. Relax.'

She was already relaxed, too relaxed, her heated pleasure almost out of control. She had never known, never dreamt it could be like this, this complete surrender to the senses. If she had imagined love between two people at all she had thought of it as a coming together of two people who shared the same interests and gradually grew to love each other to the extent of wanting to give themselves to each other. But this wasn't like that at all, and yet she couldn't think of not giving herself to Damien, wanted to share with him the one thing she had given no other man.

Damien raised his dark head to look at her with glazed eyes. 'You know I want you, Kate. You aren't going to refuse me, are you?'

Silently she shook her head, already past the point of caring that Damien Savage, the man about to make love to her in the fullest sense of the word, was someone she had met for the first time yesterday, someone she had disliked until today, despised even. None of these things seemed important here and now, only the closeness of their two bodies and the sure touch of his hands were important to her at this moment.

'Help me off with these.' He leant on his elbow as she made an effort to release the single fastening to his trousers, glancing up as she winced. 'What's the matter?' he looked concerned. 'Did I hurt you?'

She was beginning to feel embarrassed at the intensity of his gaze on her nakedness, of the glazed look in his eyes. 'It was your chin. It's rough,' she explained huskily.

'Oh damn!' He touched his chin impatiently, his eyes darkening as he looked down at her. 'God, look what I've done to your skin!' He touched one sensitive breast. 'That must have hurt like hell.' He soothed the hot reddened skin. 'Why didn't you tell me?'

Kate wished he would shut up and kiss her. She didn't want him to talk to her, it only reminded her of who he was and what he was doing to her. She looked away. 'It didn't hurt at the time.'

His smile gently mocked. 'I guess I'd better have that shave after all.' He got up from the bed. 'Don't move, I won't be long.' With a last lingering look at her he went into the adjoining bathroom.

Kate lay dazed by her own emotions. What was she *doing* here? More to the point, what was Damien doing in here with her? Already she had allowed him to spend the night in the same bed as herself—perhaps allowed wasn't quite the right word to use, she had had little choice in the matter.

But she did have a choice about letting him make love to her! And she wasn't going to wait here like a wanton. She might have been momentarily carried away by the mastery and expertise of the man, but not any more.

She had to get out of here before she disgraced herself completely. Anyway, he had said that virginity didn't interest him, and she was certainly that. Her inexperience would soon bore a man of his reputation, and she didn't intend just being another scalp added to the belt of any man.

She could hear Damien humming to himself in the bathroom as she hurriedly dressed herself, and the sound of his self-assurance only made her all the more determined to leave. She was no more to him than a diversion, someone to go to bed with during his stay in England. Well, he would find that here was one girl he wasn't going to win so easily!

She slipped quietly out of the room, collecting her overnight case from the other bedroom on her way out. She sighed with relief as the lift doors closed behind her; at least she had managed to get out of the apartment without detection.

The man Damien had addressed as Barry the night before was sitting at the reception desk. He looked up and smiled at her. 'Good morning,' he said, standing up politely.

Kate blushed. There was no familiarity in the man's voice and yet she knew she must look odd leaving the building at nine o'clock in the morning dressed in an evening gown. She could have gone to the other bedroom and put on her trouser suit, but this would have only wasted precious time, time she didn't have. 'Good morning,' she returned, her words stilted in her embarrassment.

'Would you like me to call you a taxi?' he enquired.

It was a good idea, but it would perhaps be safer to flag one down once she had got away from this apartment block, safer because she had no doubt Damien Savage would be furiously angry once he realised she had cheated on him once again. He really did have a cheek, believing she would let him make love to her after only one evening spent together. The conceit of the man!

She gave the man a bright smile. 'No, thank you. I don't have far to go.' She left before he could say any more, unwilling to be drawn into a conversation with him. She just wanted to get away from here as quickly as possible.

James' apartment wasn't too far away and it didn't take long to get there in the taxi she had managed to acquire. She would have a quick bath and change before finding some way of transporting herself back to James' country home. Perhaps she could ring him and ask him to come and fetch her. But if she did that he would want to know what had gone wrong—and she had no intention of telling him what had taken place the night before, or this morning for that matter.

The bath was so relaxing and luxurious that she spent more time over it than she had intended, lazing under the soft scented bubbles. It was so nice to just let herself relax after the terrible day she had spent yesterday, and she lay back, her head resting on the back of this large sunken bath, her hair secured on top of her head with a black velvet ribbon.

She smiled slightly at the size of the bathroom. James certainly liked to live in style, and the luxury of this sunken bath, fitted carpet, and completely mirrored walls all added to that.

'I wouldn't fall asleep in there.'

Her eyes flew open and she gasped as she saw Damien Savage lounging just inside the room, his reflection thrown back at her from the four corners of the room. She sank further below the bubbles. 'How did you get in here?'

He walked casually over to stand on the bath's edge, his leather-clad feet only inches away from her head. 'You left these in the door,' he held up the keys. 'Very careless of you.' He dropped them uncaringly into the water at her feet.

Kate sat up with a start, searching frantically about in the cooling water for the keys. 'What did you do that for? Where on earth are they?' she muttered worriedly.

Damien kicked off his shoes, sitting down on the bath's edge before slowly sliding into the water. 'I'll help you look for them.'

She gasped, her eyes opening wide with shock. 'Get out of here! I'll find the keys when I let out the water. You'll ruin your trousers,' she added desperately when he didn't seem to be listening to her.

He shrugged. 'So I'll borrow a pair of James'. I'm sure he must leave some here.'

Kate shrank back against the side of the bath, covering her bare breasts with her hands, jumping nervously as his searching hand came into contact with her leg. 'Will you get out of here!' she demanded hysterically.

'No.' His green eyes rested on her red face. 'Stop panicking, honey. I've seen you naked once this morning already.' He bent down and scooped her up in his arms, wading out of the water and into the bedroom, dripping water everywhere. He threw her down on to the bed, pinning her there with his arms. 'Now,' he said, his face only inches away from her own, 'would you mind telling me why you felt it necessary to run out on me this morning?'

'Your—your clothes!' She looked down at the wet outline her body had made on his black shirt. 'You're all wet!'

His hand tightened about her wrist. 'Answer the question, Kate.'

'Wh-what was it?' She couldn't think, his closeness unnerved her. Why had he followed her here? What was he hoping to achieve? Surely he wasn't hoping to continue where they had left off in his bedroom this morning, surely even he couldn't expect that?

'Why did you run out on me?' he repeated.

She looked away. 'You must know why.'

'Must I?'

'Yes!' she answered shortly, well aware of the dangerousness of her position lying here beneath him. 'You—you seduced me with your closeness this morning, and you're doing the same thing now. You're taking advantage of my weakness.'

His warm breath fanned her cheeks as he released her hair from the restricting ribbon with one strong hand. 'Do I make you weak?'

She pushed his hand away. 'You know you do,' she said crossly.

'I know, do I?' he mused. 'And how would I know that?'

Kate glared at him, resenting his taunting tone and the way he had complete control over her. 'You know because you're well aware of the effect you have on all women. You emit a sensuous arrogance that sends out a challenge to every woman who looks at you.'

'And you accepted that challenge, did you?' he mocked softly, his eyes passing tantalisingly over her face and body.

'No, I didn't! Look, I don't have the experience to fight men like you. I'm a complete pushover when it comes to your sophisticated type of seduction, I admit that.' She stopped fighting him. 'So if you want me you might as well get on with it—I don't have any defences left where you're concerned.'

To her surprise he started to laugh, a deep throaty sound that was very attractive. He rolled away from her. 'What a turn-off that is! I like my women willing, yes, but I don't like them uninterested.' He stood up, throwing the damp coverlet over her naked body. 'I can wait until you're ready to come to me willingly.'

'That will probably be never.' She clutched the coverlet to her.

'We'll see.' He looked down ruefully at his clinging clothing. '*Does* St Just have any clothes here I can change into?'

'In his bedroom,' she told him shortly. 'The second door on the right out of here.'

'*His* bedroom?' he taunted. 'Surely he doesn't bother to have separate rooms? You won't be allowed that luxury when you live with me. I intend to have all your nights.'

'Why did you follow me?' she quavered.

He turned briefly to look at her. 'You're mine, Kate, and I don't let go easily of what's mine.'

'I'm not yours, I don't belong to anyone!'

'Not even St Just?' he asked gratingly. 'I would have thought two years was long enough for him to think he has a lot of rights where you're concerned. And I don't like it. I'll take you back to his house when you're dressed and call back for you later this evening. You can pack your clothes and be ready to leave at eight o'clock. Don't keep me waiting, I'm not going to fight St Just over you.'

'I'm not moving in with you,' she said stubbornly. 'You attract me physically, I can't deny that. There wouldn't be much point, you know it every time you touch me. But that doesn't mean we should live together.'

'You mean because I may have habits that will annoy you?' He smiled. 'Like squeezing the toothpaste from the middle of the tube, things like that?' He shrugged. 'I've had no complaints in the past.'

'How many people have you had living with you?'

'None,' he laughingly closed the door.

Within half an hour they were on their way to James' country house, Damien wearing a pair of James' white trousers. He was a more muscular man than James and the trousers fitted snugly about his hips, emphasising the length of his thighs.

He turned to her when they reached the house, his leg curiously close to her in the confines of the car. 'Be ready to leave with me this evening, angel. I'd hate to have to make you leave. And I've been thinking about your clothes and I've decided I don't want you to bring any of them with you.'

Kate's eyes opened wide. 'You can't mean to keep me at your apartment without any clothes?' She had forgotten for the moment that she wasn't actually moving in with him, feeling only shock at his words.

'No, we'll get you some new ones before we leave for the States tomorrow, the rest can be made up for you for when we return. I don't want you to bring anything with you that St Just gave you.'

'Jealousy, Damien?'

'Jealousy,' he confirmed surprisingly, moving forward to kiss her lightly on the lips. 'I won't feel sure of you until I've made you mine. Now in you go, and tell James that I'll be by tonight to discuss the movie with him. It will only take a couple of minutes, honey, just a short conversation about shooting time and location.' His lips travelled slowly over her cheek and back to her mouth. 'Mmm,' he breathed deeply against her. 'I'll be looking forward to tonight. And this time you won't have had doctored drinks!'

Kate scrambled inelegantly out of the car, far away from the seduction in his voice and the closeness of his body. 'Goodbye, Damien,' she said hurriedly.

He put up a hand in farewell. 'See you later, angel.'

She watched him as he accelerated the car out of the driveway. He had almost had her believing that she *was* moving in with him. But she wasn't—James wouldn't allow it for one thing. At least, she hoped he wouldn't; she knew she wasn't strong enough to say no to him herself. He could be much too persuasive for an innocent like her.

CHAPTER FOUR

ONLY Sheri and James remained of the house-party of yesterday, both of them in the lounge drinking coffee as Kate let herself quietly into the room.

'Kate!' James jumped up on her arrival. 'Where have you been?'

She evaded his searching eyes. 'You know where I've been.' She moved out of his arms. 'Hello, Sheri.' She smiled at the butler as he bought her in a coffee cup. 'Thank you, Jennings.' She watched as Sheri filled the cup for her.

James waited until the butler had left before carrying on with their conversation. 'You weren't at the apartment, Kate,' he remarked quietly behind her. 'I called you several times, once last night and twice this morning.'

She tried to cover her shock at being found at so easily, smiling brightly at her brother as she accepted the coffee Sheri handed to her. 'I probably wasn't back from the party last night when you called and I was in the bath when you called this morning.'

'This morning's calls were made two hours apart,' James persisted.

'*Okay*, so I was still asleep when you made the first one.' She was starting to get agitated now.

'Stop cross-questioning the girl, James,' Sheri chided him gently. 'I know what I would have been doing after spending the evening with Damien Savage, and it wouldn't have had anything to do with sleeping.'

'Sheri!' He looked scandalised. 'This is my sister you're talking to.'

Now it was Kate's turn to look surprised. That James, who had always maintained the secrecy of their family link,

61

should brazenly announce that they were brother and sister! 'James?' She looked at him searchingly.

He put out his arm to pull Sheri against his side, looking rather bashful for the usually self-confident James. 'Er—Sheri and I are going to be married, Kate.'

She looked from one to the other of them, seeing their happiness in each other mirrored in their faces, hugging them each in turn. 'I'm so pleased for you!' she glowed at them. 'It's wonderful news. When's the wedding?'

Sheri laughed at her enthusiasm. 'Hey, give us chance to get used to the idea that there's going to be a wedding at all! I must admit to feeling apprehensive about you in the past, not knowing the connection between the two of you. Everyone thinks——'

'Everyone thinks that we're lovers,' Kate finished with a grimace. 'Damien Savage seems to be under the same misapprehension—and treats me accordingly.'

Her brother's face darkened with anger. 'What's he been saying to you?'

'Only what a lot of other people have undoubtedly been thinking,' she sighed. 'I only wish I could tell them the truth, but it's impossible. There's your mother. And we mustn't forget our father's reputation.'

James gave her a sympathetic look. 'Don't be bitter, Kate. If I thought it would do any good to announce to the world that you're my sister, then I'd do it. I know that things like illegitimacy are accepted nowadays, but if people realised that Richard St Just had fathered such a child eighteen years ago there would be a terrible scandal. Besides, as you said, there's my mother to think of. You must realise what it would do to her if it became public knowledge. It was a shock for her to learn of your existence at all, without that.'

'No more of a shock to her than it was to me.' Kate smiled wanly at Sheri. 'I'm sorry you have had to witness this, but James and I can never agree on the subject.'

'That's because he isn't the one that's illegitimate. He'd probably feel differently if it were him. Now don't scowl at me, James,' she teased him. 'I can see this from both sides. You obviously feel for your mother, but Kate is the one who has to put up with the innuendoes about the two of you. Perhaps it will stop once we're married.'

'I wouldn't count on it,' James said dryly. 'I should think it will make matters worse.'

'Not if I move out it won't,' Kate said quietly.

'Oh, but you aren't——'

'I couldn't allow——'

'Neither of you will stop me,' she interrupted. 'I realise now that it's been the mistake we've made all along. I should never have come to live with you, James, but had my own apartment. And that's exactly what I intend doing.'

'You will not!' James looked furious. 'How can I keep an eye on you if you don't live with me?'

'I'm over eighteen. I don't need your permission to move out.'

'That's because you aren't going to. You're staying right here. Let the gossips say what they like, I don't give a damn.'

'Sheri?' she looked at her future sister-in-law.

'I agree with James. This is your home, you don't have to be forced out by gossip.'

'And if I want to move out? If I want to be free to choose my own friends, live my own life?'

James snorted his disgust. 'Like that insipid Nigel Humphries, I suppose?'

Kate looked uncomfortable. 'Maybe not like Nigel—I think you were right about him. He only wanted to be friends with me because he thought I might get you to help with his career.'

'I won't say I told you so,' he said, instantly contradicting himself. 'And you aren't moving out. I forbid it.'

'James!' Now it was Sheri's turn to look shocked. 'I agree

with you about Kate not moving out, but you have no right to order her about. You must consider her feelings in all this.'

'Thank you, Sheri,' Kate smiled at her before turning back to James. 'I do want to move out. I think it would be for the best. It has nothing to do with your marriage, in fact I want to move out in the next few days.'

James' grey eyes narrowed suspiciously. 'Does this have anything to do with Damien Savage, with the fact that you went out with him yesterday evening and I wasn't able to reach you either then or this morning?'

Kate looked away, her face fiery red. 'I don't know what you mean.'

His stance was challenging. 'I mean has your decision to leave anything to do with Damien Savage.'

'Certainly not,' she replied truthfully.

'Where were you last night?' he asked softly.

'I was at the apartment, I already told you that.' Her temper threatened to overflow at her guilt in lying to him. 'Don't keep questioning me, James!'

'I keep questioning you because I think you're lying to me,' he sighed. 'If I thought my persuading you to go out with Damien had led you to—to——'

'It didn't.' But it nearly had! How near the truth he was. Damien Savage had a magnetism that was positively lethal, drugging to the senses.

Sheri reached up to kiss James fleetingly on the lips. 'I'm not running out on you, honey, but I do have that plane to catch. I'll go and get my things together. Be gentle with her, hmm?'

'She's my sister, Sheri. My kid sister.'

Sheri smiled encouragingly at her before turning back to her fiancé. 'She looks quite grown up to me, James. Quite old enough to make her own decisions.'

'Thank you once again, Sheri,' Kate said gratefully.

'That's enough of that,' her brother interrupted gruffly. 'I won't have the two of you ganging up on me already.'

Sheri laughed, flicking back her shoulder-length hair. 'I'll just go and get my things.'

'All right,' he kissed her lingeringly on the lips. 'Don't be long. We only have an hour and a half to get you to the airport, although why you can't break that damned modelling contract and stay here with me I don't know. We could get married almost immediately.'

'My, you're impulsive when you want to be! I have to honour that contract because I'm a professional model, I have my reputation to think of. Besides, you have three more months' run in that play to go yet. I intend for us to have a proper honeymoon, not a few days snatched together between working.'

James grimaced. 'You see how she's beginning to nag me already.'

'Shame!' His fiancée laughingly left the room.

Kate smiled. 'I am pleased for you, James. Sheri is exactly right for you.'

He looked at her closely. 'You're sure you don't mind? I did intend talking to you about it before I did anything as serious as proposing to her, but I just seemed to go ahead before I could talk to you.'

She grinned. 'She just swept you off your feet,' she teased.

He looked sheepish. 'More or less,' he admitted. 'I just found myself asking her to marry me.'

She hugged him, realising just how easy it was to be swept away by your own emotions. But as far as she was concerned it had been a case of physical attraction, nothing as dramatic as love. In a way she wished it had been, at least then she could have excused her reaction to Damien, could have accepted it even. As it was she was utterly confused.

'You'd better get yourself ready if you're going to the airport,' she suggested easily. 'I'm just going to my room to change.'

'Okay. But, Kate ...' he paused, 'you didn't mean it about moving out, did you?'

She felt almost guilty at the hurt she could see in his eyes. 'I did mean it, James. It isn't that I don't love you, I just feel I should live my own life, stand on my own two feet.'

'Who's been putting these ideas into your head?' he asked shrewdly.

'No one,' she denied. 'It was just something someone said to me.'

'What did they say to you?'

She moved uncomfortably. 'What does it matter what was actually said, they were right.'

'They?' he prompted.

Kate ignored the question. 'I'm just vegetating here. I don't work, I have nothing to occupy me at all. I could— well, I could become a model like Sheri,' she said excitedly. 'Or I could try acting, like you. Damien said——' she broke off guiltily.

'Yes?' James queried mildly. 'Just what did Damien say? I take it he's the one who's been handing out unwelcome advice?'

Her brown eyes flashed. 'You take it right. And it wasn't exactly advice.'

'I can imagine,' he said dryly.

'But he is right, you have to admit that.'

'Maybe. And what were you about to say he said?'

'He thinks I may be very photogenic,' she admitted. 'He asked me to go for a screen test tomorrow.'

'Oh yes?' He looked sceptical.

Kate grinned at the look on his face. 'I reacted the same way you are, but he really was serious. He thinks I could be a big star.'

James frowned worriedly. 'I don't want that for you, Kate. It isn't as easy for women in this business as it is for men. I don't think our father would appreciate my allowing you to enter this disreputable profession either—his words not mine. Did you agree to go?'

She shook her head, her long hair swinging about her shoulders. 'No, I'm of the same opinion as you. That sort of life isn't for me, one actor in the family is enough. Actually, he seemed quite pleased that I had refused.'

'Did he indeed?' James bit his lip thoughtfully. 'I wonder why that was, after he'd gone to the trouble of offering it to you. Believe me, if he said you would be good then you would be. He knows what he's talking about. I can't say I approve of the idea myself, but you may be a fool to turn him down.'

'I already have.' She stopped on her way to her room. 'By the way, Damien said he'd be over later tonight. Something to do with the film, I think.'

James' face brightened. 'He's given me the part?'

She nodded, giving him a mischievous grin. 'But that isn't what he wants to talk to you about. I think he probably wants to discuss your co-star with you.'

'My co-star?' His brow cleared. 'For the part of Rogers, I suppose. Who has he chosen?'

'Oh, I couldn't tell you that, it would be breaking a confidence,' she laughed at the consternation on his face. 'Damien wouldn't like it, he's the director after all.'

'Damn Damien! Tell me.'

'I'm not sure I should,' she teased. 'Anyway, you won't like it.'

He caught up with her at the door and swung her round to face him, smiling unwillingly at the mischief in her face. 'It has to be someone pretty bad for you to find it so amusing.' The smile faded from his face. 'Oh no, I've just realised ... It's Matt Strange, isn't it? The rotten sneaking bast—swine!' he amended. 'Damien deliberately let me think—God, he's devious! I even let you go out with him yesterday on the strength of it and all the time he had us picked out as a partnership. I should have realised, Matt's brash overbearing nature is perfect for the part of Rogers. It just never occurred to me. And that's what he's coming here to talk about?'

Kate turned away. 'I think so.'

'He isn't usually so considerate of people's feelings.' His steel-grey eyes narrowed. 'Are you sure he isn't coming to see you?'

'He——' She licked her lips and then blushed as she remembered Damien's comment about this unconscious habit of hers. 'Well, he may be,' she said at last.

'Which means he is,' said James with finality. 'How did your evening with the great man go? Did he make any passes at you?'

She wouldn't exactly call them passes. He hadn't been making a pass at her this morning when he had carried her naked from her bath; his intent had been clearly defined as sexual, nothing so insipid as a mere pass. But she couldn't tell James about that, he would be furious. He might even refuse to star in the film, and she couldn't let that happen.

'Not a single one,' she denied. 'Quite a let-down for Damien Savage.'

'You're sure he isn't coming back tonight to try again?'

She tried her best to look nonchalant. 'Do his type usually try twice?'

'If they want something badly enough I would say yes. And he made no secret of his attraction to you. Not even one pass?' he persisted.

'Well ... maybe a little one.' James would become suspicious if she denied it completely. 'But I rebuffed him. I told you before I went, I don't like the man.' That wasn't strictly true now. She was frightened of him now rather than felt dislike, frightened of the feelings he could arouse in her. 'The airport, James,' she reminded him. 'You mustn't let Sheri miss her plane.'

'She wouldn't go at all if I had my way,' he muttered. 'But I suppose I should go and change. We'll talk when I get back, or rather I'll try to talk you out of leaving me.'

She sighed. 'I don't think you'll succeed. It's time I grew up, time I stopped depending on you for everything, including protection from the outside world. I can't be a child for ever, James.'

'One evening out with Damien Savage and you come to these conclusions. I wish I'd never let you go with him now.'

So did Kate, but for very different reasons. She thought of him as she changed, she seemed to be able to think of little else. He had shaken her out of her dream-world as nothing else could have done, had brought her to an awareness of how shallow her friendships with Nigel and men like him had been. None of them could have brought her to life with just the look in their eyes or the smallest touch of their hands.

But it was Damien's experience that enabled him to do that, the vast amount of women he had known before her. If she had given in to him, as she had wanted to, she would just have been another woman in the long line of females that had enhanced his life, just another casual relationship.

He had invited her to live with him, but how long would that have lasted? And even then could she have been sure she was the only woman in his life? It didn't seem likely; he didn't appear to be the constant type, his affairs lasting a couple of months at most.

But what could she say to him tonight to make him leave her alone? How could she get him to leave without making a scene? She certainly didn't want to admit to James just how far things had gone between them, or the attraction they felt for each other that was the destruction of any ideals she might have had about love and marriage.

*

She must have dozed by the pool, because it was quite late in the afternoon by the time she was awakened by a polite cough from Jennings, their butler. She smiled at him sleepily, and sat up lazily. 'Yes, Jennings?'

He held himself stiffly correct, reminding Kate of a character out of a P. G. Wodehouse story. She felt sure he must be highly shocked by the behaviour of some of James' friends, although in no way would he ever show it, he was much too polite for that. 'There's a gentleman to see Mr St Just, Miss Darwood. I have informed him that Mr St Just is not at home at the moment and so he requested to see you instead.'

Damien! It had to be him. Lord, he was early. He had said this evening some time. What was she going to do now? What could she do, she would have to ask him in. She put a hand to her hair, looking down in horror at the bikini she wore. God, she must look a mess, she couldn't see him looking like this.

'Miss Darwood?' Jennings was still waiting for her answer.

'Show him into the lounge, Jennings,' she said finally. 'I'll be there in a few minutes.'

'Yes, miss.'

She scrambled off the lounger, picking up her sunglasses and book to hurry along the poolside to the house. She wasn't even halfway there when a man came strolling out of the house, casually dressed in a brown shirt and cream trousers, a man completely sure of his effect on the opposite sex. He gave Kate that wicked grin that she detested, leering at her with those blue eyes that stripped away what little clothing she had on.

'Mr Strange,' she said stiffly, holding herself as aloof as it was possible to do in a minute black bikini. 'James isn't here, I'm afraid.' She would even have preferred Damien to this hateful man, would have welcomed him even.

He smiled at her. 'I know that, Kate. But I can wait.'

Not with her he couldn't! She didn't like him one little bit, although he seemed to be very popular with the public, a fact that had always puzzled her. He was conceited to the point of making her feel physically sick, with about as much charm as an over-sexed ape.

The first couple of times she had met him he had tried, unsuccessfully, to get her to go out with him. She felt sure it was only because he considered she belonged to James and he couldn't bear to think that any woman was immune to him. Well, here was one woman who was; he sickened her utterly.

'I'm not sure what time he'll be returning,' she lied, well aware that James intended being back for dinner.

'That's okay, I don't mind waiting,' he returned smoothly.

'He could be a long time,' she insisted.

'I have plenty of time,' he smiled. 'You could even invite me to dinner.'

The audacity of the man! 'But I——'

'Thanks, I'd love to. Let's sit down, shall we?' he indicated the chairs beside the pool. 'It's not often I get to see you on your own. I must say it gave me quite a surprise to see you with Damien last night. I thought James only allowed for competition like Nigel Humphries,' he taunted. 'Damien's in a class all of his own.'

She knew that—oh yes, she knew that. 'I accompanied Mr Savage to your party because he'd only just arrived in the country and needed a partner.'

Matt Strange snorted his disbelief. 'He only has to snap his fingers and the girls come running, so I'm sure that isn't the case. I wasn't even sure you would still be staying here.'

'Why shouldn't I be?'

He shrugged. 'Sit down and I'll tell you.'

'I—I can't. I have to change.'

His eyes ran over her tanned body appraisingly. 'Don't

bother on my account, I like you as you are.'

She could imagine he did! At twenty-seven he was the biggest lecher she had ever had the misfortune to meet. She couldn't even understand why he needed to be like this; he was very good-looking in a rugged sort of way, with his blond hair, shrewd blue eyes, and a tough muscled body. If only he weren't so obnoxious in other ways!

Instant stardom two years ago had probably done that to him. It couldn't be easy to be suddenly thrust into the public eye, to be recognised and looked at wherever you went. James had become accustomed to this adoration over a period of twenty years, this man had had two years to come to terms with it, and apparently he hadn't yet done so.

But why should she be making excuses for his behaviour? She didn't like him or his attitude towards women, and nothing he did could change that. 'I was just going in to change when you arrived,' she insisted. 'If you'll excuse me for a few minutes.'

'Why don't you sit down, Kate? I'm not going to harm you. I only came here to talk.' Again he indicated that she should sit down.

'Oh, all right,' she agreed. 'Just for a few minutes, then I really must go to my room.' She sat down. 'Why did you want to see James?'

'No particular reason. I just thought that as we were shortly going to be working together I should try and improve diplomatic relations between us. James and I have had our disagreements in the past, a couple of them about you,' he grinned at her. 'But that's all over now, now that you and James aren't—well, now that you're no longer James' exclusive property.'

Kate frowned. 'What does that have to do with anything? And why should you think that anyway?'

'James has always given anyone he doesn't approve of who comes within touching distance of you the hands-off signal. But that can no longer apply, not after your little evening out with Damien. I originally came here to see James,' he added, 'but in a way I'm glad he isn't here, it gives me the opportunity to ask you out to dinner with me this evening. Will you come?'

Kate shook her head. 'I'm sorry, I can't do that, not this evening.' Not any time if she could help it!

'Then how about tomorrow?'

'No, I'm sorry,' again she refused, beginning to feel hot all over at the way his eyes slid over her body. He made her skin crawl. 'I'm not sure what James' plans are for tomorrow.'

He raised one eyebrow and lounged back comfortably in the chair. 'Does it matter what he's doing? I would have thought you could make your own arrangements now.'

'You seem to have the wrong impression about me, Mr Strange. James and are I friends, nothing more. I've always been able to go out with whom I chose.'

'I see.' His blue eyes narrowed. 'That isn't the impression James gives. Does that mean that in the past it was your decision not to go out with me?'

She realised the trap she had set for herself too late. 'I—well, I—— Yes, I suppose so.' She fidgeted with her sunglasses, embarrassed at her disclosure.

'But you didn't feel the same reluctance where Damien Savage was concerned?' he asked softly.

Kate could tell by the dangerous glitter in his blue eyes that he was fast losing his temper, and he was well known for his rages, often made in public, and splashed across the front of the daily newspapers. She didn't welcome being the cause of one of those rages. 'No,' she said softly, watching him closely.

'So you've dropped James for Damien?'

'Do you think it likely that I would still be living here if that were the case?' She shook her head. 'I told you, you have the wrong idea about myself and James. And I went out with Damien Savage for one night only. It won't be repeated.'

'Then why won't you come out with me?'

Because she didn't want to! Any normal man would have realised that by now. But not this man; he couldn't accept disinterest, believing himself to be completely attractive to all women. She looked pointedly at her wrist-watch. 'It's getting late, Mr Strange. I must get out of this bikini.'

'You haven't answered my question yet, Kate. But I can wait. You're worth waiting for. Go ahead and change, I'll wait here.'

This plan didn't please Kate at all. 'I could be some time,' she discouraged.

'That's okay, I'm in no hurry to leave.'

And he didn't look as if he was, sitting quite relaxed as he looked up at her now standing figure. 'In that case you may as well go into the lounge and help yourself to a drink. I'll be as quick as I can,' she told him crossly.

'I told you, I'm in no hurry.' He too stood up. 'Don't bother to show me the way, I know where to go.'

He didn't, or he would have left completely. She didn't want him here. He must have a skin like a rhinoceros if he didn't realise that. She sorted through her wardrobe, trying to find something that wouldn't draw too much attention to her; Matt Strange was interested enough without that.

She discarded the bikini, donning a silk robe in preparation of taking her shower. She hoped James arrived home soon; Matt Strange was getting too intimate for comfort, and he wasn't going to take the answer no to his invitation out to dinner. She absolutely refused to accompany another man she had no wish to go out with.

'Very nice!'

She turned sharply to see Matt Strange standing in the open doorway of her bedroom, a glass of some amber fluid in his hand. 'What are you——'

He moved forward into the room, closing the door softly behind him. 'If anything you look more seductive in that silk thing than you did in your minute bikini.'

To Kate he looked totally menacing. 'I don't remember inviting you into my bedroom.' She made an effort to remain cool, she wouldn't give him the satisfaction of seeing how he unnerved her.

'Do I need an invitation?' All the time he was moving closer.

'I would have thought so.' She watched him warily, backing slowly away from him until she felt herself come up against the bedroom wall.

He put down his empty glass on her white dressing-table, moving forward to pin her to the wall with a hand either side of her head. 'Don't act the innocent with me, Kate. I know exactly what you are.' He lowered his body against hers. 'And I think it's my turn now.' He bent his head to kiss her creamy throat.

She couldn't repress her shiver of revulsion at the touch of his lips to her skin, squirming away from him but not getting very far with his hands restraining her. 'Let go of me!' she snapped between gritted teeth, trying to stop herself from crying out. 'If you don't let go of me I swear I'll scream the house down,' she promised vehemently.

He laughed mockingly against her throat. 'You know you like it—your sort always do. If you like to fight, then we'll fight. I don't mind.'

Kate gasped her shock. 'You're disgusting, absolutely disgusting! I meant it about screaming. If you touch me once more I'll let out the biggest yell you've ever heard!'

'I don't believe you.' His lips continued their downward path.

Her scream was stifled halfway through by his hand placed roughly over her mouth. She glared her dislike of him, the gold flecks in her eyes clearly showing her hatred of him and his treatment of her.

'So you want to play rough, do you?' he growled at her, an ugly look of anger on his flushed face. 'Okay, so we'll play rough.' He picked her up and threw her on the bed. 'You're the most provocative little bitch I've ever met, and I intend to have you!'

'I don't think so,' remarked a voice Kate instantly recognised, quickly wrapping the robe about her naked body where it had come awry by Matt Strange's rough handling of her, looking up thankfully to see Damien Savage standing just inside the room. 'If you're a very wise man, Strange,' he continued, dangerously soft, 'you'll just leave quietly.'

The younger man looked at him challengingly. 'And if I choose not to?'

'Then we'll just go outside and settle this matter another way.'

Matt Strange looked down at Kate, who was now shivering with reaction. 'I don't think you're worth the bother,' he said tauntingly. 'Maybe I was wrong and my time hasn't come yet.' He looked up at Damien. 'I can wait until you've finished with her.'

The next thing Kate knew he was lying at her feet, blood pouring from his nose. The look on his face could only be described as ugly and she flinched from that look. Suddenly he smiled. 'She simply isn't worth it, Damien. I'll just leave before this whole thing gets out of control. See you around, Kate, Damien.'

There was a stunned silence after he had left, until Kate broke into loud choking sobs. She felt dirty and degraded, felt as if she wanted to scrub every inch of her body to erase Matt Strange's touch. She sensed Damien standing beside her and turned to bury her face against him, his arm about her shoulders holding her close.

'It's all right, honey,' he said softly. 'It's all over now.'

'Oh, Damien,' she clung to him. 'It was awful, awful!'

He smoothed back her hair with a gentle hand, a trace of

anger still burning in his green eyes. 'I know, honey. I felt murderous when I walked in here and saw you with him. I wouldn't have realised what was going on if I hadn't heard your scream. I arrived a few minutes ago and Jennings went off in search of you.'

She was still shivering with fright. 'Oh, Damien, if you hadn't come in ...'

'But I did.' He tilted her chin to smile down at her. 'Now get yourself dressed and I'll go and reassure Jennings that you're all right.' He gently touched her lips with his own.

Her mouth bloomed and clung to his, her arms passing up around his neck to hold him to her. He kissed her back for several long seconds before firmly putting her away from him. She looked at him with hurt bewildered eyes. 'Damien?'

'Get dressed, Kate,' he told her almost harshly. 'I'll be waiting for you in the lounge.'

Her feelings of rejection were very acute after he had left her and the tears flowed more freely. Within the space of a few minutes she had almost been made love to against her will and then coldly rebuffed by the man she—— By the man she *what*? By the man she loved? Surely not. She couldn't love Damien Savage. She just couldn't!

She was pale and composed by the time she entered the lounge fifteen minutes later, freshly showered and dressed in lime green trousers and matching vest-top. Damien stood up at her entrance, searching her pale features sympathetically.

'Feeling better?' he asked softly.

'Yes, thank you.' She helped herself to a cup of coffee he had ordered. 'Thank you for your help earlier on,' she added primly.

'You already thanked me, with deeds rather than words. I prefer those sort of thanks.'

She looked at him uncertainly. 'I don't understand ...'

'Come here and kiss me and you will.'

'Come over there and kiss you?' she repeated breathlessly, feeling weak at the suggestion.

'Yes,' he said shortly. 'Is that so hard to do?'

'No, I—— It isn't hard at all.' She went to him willingly, putting her arms about his waist, her head resting on his chest, hearing the steady beat of his heart. She sighed her pleasure, feeling strangely safe in his arms, even though she knew he wanted her as much as Matt Strange had, maybe even more. She didn't feel repulsion in Damien's arms, only a longing she didn't wholly understand.

He reached up to free her hair and smooth it down about her shoulders. 'Always leave your hair loose when you're with me,' he ordered. 'I can't stand to see such glorious hair hidden away.'

'Yes, Damien.'

He gave a husky laugh. 'I can see I'll have to rescue you from sex-crazed attackers more often! It makes you much more submissive.' His told tightened as she repressed a shudder. 'We have to talk about it, angel, or else you'll blow it up in your mind out of all proportion.'

'But it—it was so horrible.' She stiffened as she heard the sound of voice outside. 'I think James has just arrived home.' She went to move out of his arms.

His hold remained firm. 'Stay where you are. Perhaps when James sees you in my arms he'll get the message. I take it you haven't told him about us?'

'No. But——'

'Then stay here and let him draw his own conclusions.'

'No, I—I can't!' She wrenched out of his arms just as the door opened to admit James.

'Ah, Damien,' he greeted the other man. 'So pleased you could make it. I hope you've been looking after our guest, Kate.' He saw the coffee-tray. 'Ah, yes, I can see you have. Well, I'm glad you're here now, Damien, to drink a toast with us.'

Damien frowned. 'A toast? Are you celebrating something?'

'Mm,' James grinned. 'Haven't you told him about the wedding, Kate?'

'What wedding?' Damien asked sharply.

James put his arm about Kate's shoulders. 'Why, my wedding, old man,' he answered happily.

Kate looked in dismay from her brother's face over to Damien's, well aware that James had deliberately implied that it was the two of them who were marrying. And from the furiously accusing look Damien was giving her, it had worked.

CHAPTER FIVE

HER heart sank with dismay. James was only trying to protect her, she realised that, but he had chosen the wrong time to do it. She didn't want to be protected from Damien any more, she just wanted to let things happen between them.

But she could tell by the determination on James' face that he had no intention of allowing that to happen, that he would do anything to stop it. He grinned down at her now, the humour not quite reaching his grey eyes. 'Yes, I've finally given in. I've realised that I just can't live without her.'

'A bit sudden, isn't it?' Damien snapped curtly.

'Not that sudden. She's been in my life a long time now. Besides, I think that once you realise there's one woman you don't want to share with anyone else then that's the time to give in to fate.'

'I see.' Damien's eyes ripped into Kate with a violence that made her wince. 'And you've just suddenly realised that?'

James grinned. 'Oh, not suddenly. I've been realising my fate was decided for some time now. This weekend made my mind up for me.'

'Did it just?' Damien's mouth turned back in a sneer.

James was prevented from answering by the entrance of the butler. 'Yes, Jennings?'

'Telephone, sir. It's Miss Anderson, from America.'

'Thank you, Jennings. I'll take it in the study,' he dismissed the man. 'Excuse me, I shouldn't be too long.'

There was a long awkward silence after he had left the room, with Kate giving Damien surreptitious glances from

80

under lowered lids. James had been very clever in his deceit—he hadn't actually lied once, just omitted the name of his bride. He had made Damien blazingly angry, and she really couldn't blame him for feeling like that. And what on earth must he think of her?

He soon told her. 'You used me, Kate,' he said forcefully.

'Damien, it isn't like it looks.'

'Isn't like it looks, damn it to hell!' he burst out fiercely. 'My God, what a game you've been having with us, playing us off one against the other.'

Kate gasped. 'I've done nothing of the sort! I wouldn't do such a thing.'

He gave a harsh laugh. 'What a bloody fool I've been! I fell for your little game like a prize idiot.'

'There was no little game!' she insisted, realising she wasn't going to convince him. Damien wasn't willing to believe her and that was half the battle. No matter what she said now he wouldn't listen, he didn't want to.

'Of course there damn well was. You're quite a clever little girl on the quiet, aren't you? I should have known yesterday when I heard the two of you declaring your love for each other. I didn't stand a chance of getting you to move in with me, you just used the fact that I desired you to get St Just to propose.'

'I did not!'

'It was a good scheme too, it obviously paid off. No wonder you were unwilling to let me make love to you. That didn't enter into your plans, did it?'

'There was no plan! If you'll just let me explain.' But what could she explain? The secret of her birth wasn't only hers to give.

'You're not explaining anything to me, honey. I think you've already done enough. I suppose Matt Strange was part of your scheme too, just to let James know that even though he's proposed he doesn't actually have that ring on your finger yet. I'm sorry it was me and not James who came in and broke up that pretty little scene. I realise I shouldn't have been here yet.'

Kate gasped her anger. 'Are you trying to say I arranged that—that attack this afternoon? Is that what you're saying?'

He shrugged his broad shoulders. 'Maybe not quite the way it happened. Matt just happens to be slightly more persistent than I am. He won't take no for an answer.'

'Neither will you,' she accused hotly.

'But I did—twice. I shouldn't have listened to you either, you were at my mercy this morning. I should have taken you, at least then I wouldn't have this aching feeling in my stomach. I've taken more cold showers over you the last couple of days than over any other woman. And I don't like to admit defeat, but even I draw the line at married women.'

'But I'm not marrying James,' she tried to tell him.

'You don't have to keep up this reluctance with me,' he sneered. 'James has already proposed. I just hope he realises what a little schemer you are. He won't have an easy time of it married to you, no man would.'

'You were willing to have me living with you,' she pointed out.

'But I wasn't going to marry you,' he said scathingly. 'You've been very clever to trap him into marriage.'

'I didn't trap him into anything!' God, he could be so hurtful when thwarted.

Damien smiled slightly. 'You didn't need to, you just denied him the one thing he wanted. Even I might have been prepared to marry you to get that.'

'You might?' she asked breathlessly.

'I might. Unfortunately James got there first, and I've never fought for any woman. Poor James, he had to be the one you said no to.' He shook his head.

'What do you mean?'

'Just how many lovers have you had?' he demanded.

'Why, none.'

'None!' he scoffed. 'You don't respond like an innocent, in fact I'm sure you're not. You have a good body and you know it, using it to your advantage. James must be going insane living with you like this—I would have taken you by force by now.'

'I'm sure you would!'

'You can bet on it.'

Kate was about to answer him when James came back into the room, making it impossible for them to carry on with their conversation. James couldn't know quite the scene he had just interrupted and he apparently didn't notice the tense atmosphere that existed between them, smiling broadly as he turned to face them.

'Jennings is just bringing the champagne,' he said brightly.

Kate was too choked to say anything. Damien must think her really devious to imagine she could do all the things he was accusing her of—to imagine she would deliberately use him and Matt Strange to get James to propose to her, to get any man to propose to her. The fact that James was her brother was irrelevant, Damien believed her to be capable of such deceit, that was all that seemed to matter to her at the moment.

Damien shook his head. 'Not for me, thanks. I have to be going now.'

'But we haven't discussed the film yet,' James protested.

'Kate must have told you all that seems important at the moment. All the rest can wait, we have quite a few months to shooting time. I'll be in touch.'

'Let me get Jennings to show you out.'

'I can find my own way, thanks, I found my way in. I think you should ask Kate about that, James. Ask her what she was doing in Matt Strange's arms when I arrived.' Damien paused at the door. 'And while you're at it I should ask her whose bed she slept in last night, and the circumstances behind us taking a bath together at your apartment this morning. Oh, and I must say I liked your choice of bath colour, I've always liked bottle-green.'

James' eyes had widened with shock and disbelief. 'Kate!' His look demanded that she explain.

'God, you're a swine, Damien!' she choked at him.

'Sure I am,' he agreed tauntingly. 'But I just don't see why you should have things all your own way.'

'Kate, is all this true?' Her brother looked at her sharply.

There was no mistaking the bewilderment in his voice, and Kate blushed a furious red. She could try denying everything, but the basic outline of what Damien had said was true. She *had* spent the night in his bed, in his arms in fact, and they had been in the bath together this morning. It all sounded very damning, and Damien knew that.

'Doesn't her silence tell you it is?' Damien put in dryly. 'I'll be in touch, James. Goodbye, Kate. And thanks for last night, I enjoyed every moment of it.'

'Why, you——'

'Cool it, James,' he said abruptly. 'I agree with Matt Strange, she isn't worth it.' He didn't give Kate another glance, but slammed out of the room.

'Explain, Kate!' James' look was grim.

She shrugged helplessly. 'What is there to explain? Damien's already said it all.'

'You mean it's true?'

She shook her head. 'Not the way he put it, no.'

Her brother looked stern. 'Then tell me just how it was, starting with last night.'

Kate took a deep breath and gathered her thoughts together. 'Last night Damien took me back to his apartment——'

'But you were supposed to go to mine!'

'Damien had other plans,' she sighed. 'Just let me explain, James. Right—well, he decided that it was a waste of time going to your apartment, and as I was only going to shower and change I had to admit it was too. Everything was fine until it came to going home. He went straight back to his apartment and I wasn't really in any fit state to protest too much when he started to kiss me. He is very attractive, James, overpoweringly sensual, and I wasn't a match for that. Besides, I'd had a couple of drinks at Matt Strange's and——'

'He got you drunk!' James exclaimed angrily. 'Of all the——'

'No, no, he didn't do that,' she interrupted hurriedly. 'He wasn't even with me when I drank them, he and Matt had gone off somewhere to talk. Anyway, by the time we got back to his place the drinks were starting to take effect.'

His hands clenched into fists. 'And he took advantage of you in that state? I didn't think even he would stoop that low!'

'He didn't. Will you let me finish, James, and stop jumping to conclusions!'

'All right,' he agreed grudgingly.

'Thank you. Now I'm not saying he wouldn't have made love to me—he made it very clear that that was his intention. James!' she admonished as she could see him about to interrupt yet again. 'As I was saying, he made no secret of the fact that he wanted me. And he would probably have got me too if I hadn't passed out.'

'My God! Just how much had you had to drink?'

'That's just it, as far as I was aware I'd had a couple of Martini and lemonades. Well, you know what a long drink they are, and I always like lots of lemonade. Well, apparently the barman had been doctoring them with large measures of vodka. The fresh air finally finished me off, and by the time we got to Damien's I was having trouble thinking straight, let alone resisting him.'

'So how did you get into his bed? I take it that was what he meant just now?'

Kate nodded. 'He put me there.'

'I see.' James bit his bottom lip. 'And when you woke up?'

She blushed. 'I was alone. But—well, he—he said he'd slept in the bed with me. And he—he started to——'

'Yes, yes!' he said tersely. 'I don't want to hear all the details of his practised seduction, just tell me if he actually made love to you.'

'No. He—he went to shave and I—I crept out while he was out of the room.'

'And the bath together?'

She still blushed at the thought of it. 'That isn't quite the way it seems either. When I crept out I went to your apartment. I was in the bath when Damien walked in. Oh, it's all so embarrassing, James. I don't want to talk about it any more. Nothing happened, no matter how much he implied it did. And Matt Strange can be explained even more simply—he made one of his usual passes and Damien came in and put a stop to it.'

'You've had quite a weekend, haven't you?' The tension started to leave his body. 'I shouldn't have let you go out with him. I should have known better. He isn't to be trusted.'

'I liked him, James,' she explained.

'Did you indeed? He liked you too, he was furious just now when he thought I was going to marry you.'

'Of course he was—he thinks I used him to get you to propose. He was being deliberately cruel just now when he revealed those things to you. As my future husband you could be expected to protest loudly at my conduct.'

'As your brother I can be expected to protest just as loudly.' His face relaxed into a smile. 'But if you say you're all right I'll try to get over it. You realise that this just increases my conviction that it isn't a good idea for you to live alone?'

'Oh, James!' she pouted.

'You aren't safe left alone. I've put Damien off for the moment, but once he realises that it's Sheri I'm marrying he could just be back.'

That was what she was hoping. Oh, she didn't want to become the latest in the long line of women in his life, but she would like to get to know him better. Her feelings had become more involved with him than with any other man she had ever known, her initial hostility turning to a burning curiosity to know more about him.

She felt the age-old longings of woman to be the one to tame the rogue male. And Damien was certainly that. He felt responsible to no one and gave the impression he never would be. A man alone, and intending to remain that way.

'He may be,' she admitted, 'but I would doubt it. He told me he never chases after any woman.'

'I don't suppose he needs to,' James said dryly.

'Exactly. So I'll be perfectly safe from him if I move into a flat of my own.'

'No, Kate,' he refused adamantly.

'Well, how about if I move in with someone else?' She laughed as his face darkened. 'Female, James, female!'

His brow cleared. 'Oh, I see. Mm, I suppose that's an idea. Do you have anyone in mind?'

'No, but I could advertise,' realising he was weakening.

So it was that three months later Kate found herself sharing an apartment with Josie Walker, a lighthearted girl who giggled incessantly but who had a very strong sense of moral behaviour, much to James' relief. Some of the replies they had received for Kate's future flatmate had been quite impossible, and James had refused to even contemplate most of them.

But Josie had been an instant hit with both of them, although she had been a trifle overawed at meeting the famous James St Just. She didn't seem to find it odd that James more or less interviewed her, blossoming shyly under his practised charm. Josie was a girl of twenty, sharing a flat with four other girls at the moment, but as an only child she found the constant companionship tended to make her feel claustrophobic after a while.

They had moved into the apartment James miraculously found for them three weeks previously, and although Kate missed the luxury of being waited on she revelled in the freedom of not reporting back to James after every move she made.

Poor James, he had been so busy of late that he hadn't been able to keep his usual brotherly eye on her. He had had the run of his play to finish and was also trying to organise his wedding to Sheri before they began shooting Damien Savage's film, declaring he wanted at least a month's honeymoon before he began work again.

Josie handed her the skirt to her black velvet suit, nodding her approval as Kate smoothed it on over her slim hips. The pale russet-coloured blouse was tucked in at the waist and once she had on the jacket it should be suitable attire for a wedding.

'Are you sure you won't come, Josie? Not even to the reception?' Kate began to brush her long hair.

Josie shook her head, her own long black hair secured at her nape with a wooden slide, her slim body clothed in denims and a long-sleeved smock-top. She was a pretty girl, very vivacious, with laughing deep blue eyes. 'I wouldn't feel comfortable in the midst of all those film stars and models.'

'Most of them are pretty normal.' Kate grinned as she said this; she could think of a couple of them that were a bit weird.

'No, I don't think I will come. It's very nice of Mr St Just to ask me, but I don't think Paul would like it.' Paul was her managing director boss, quite a young one at thirty, and she had high hopes of their working relationship developing on to a more personal level.

'How are things going in that direction?' asked Kate.

Josie took her hairbrush and began to brush the back of Kate's hair for her. 'Well, he's actually got round to asking me out to dinner this evening. That's partly why I'm not going out this afternoon. I'm going to spend the time getting myself ready to impress him tonight. I'm going to give him the full treatment—face pack, hairdo, full make-up, and a new dress.'

'Poor man won't know what's hit him,' Kate chuckled, satisfied that her hair was smoothed out over her jacket. She always wore her hair loose now. It took more looking after this way, but she clung to the fact that Damien liked it like this.

Damien. She had thought of him a lot the last few months, of the way he had kissed and caressed her, of his strong lithe body pressed close against her own. James had told her that Damien had come back into the country the week before, but although she had visited James a couple of times Damien hadn't been there either time.

'He'll love every minute of it,' giggled Josie.

'You're probably right,' Kate laughed too. Josie was fun and Kate really enjoyed living with her. They often stayed up late at night just chatting together and drinking coffee. Josie had a way of never being tired or bad-tempered, and she made Kate feel the same way. She stepped back, looking at Josie for approval. 'How do I look?'

'Great,' Josie enthused. 'I wish I had that lovely fiery hair.'

'You wouldn't if you had the temper too.' Kate glanced at her wrist-watch. 'The taxi's probably waiting downstairs. I'll have to go now.'

'Have fun!'

Kate wasn't sure that was going to be possible. James' friends weren't all her friends, and while she might like some of them, there were a lot of these people she would rather not be left alone with. And James would be much too preoccupied with his new bride to spare the time to look after her. James and Sheri would be leaving fairly early; they were flying to Venice for the start of their honeymoon before going on to further explore Europe, so perhaps she wouldn't have to stay at the reception too long herself.

The wedding was being held quietly at a register office in London, only twenty or so guests actually invited to this, but hundreds of people to the reception at one of London's most exclusive hotels, a huge banqueting room being used for the purpose. Kate was one of the witnesses to the wedding, so she couldn't be late. Sheri's brother was the other witness.

They were all waiting for her when she arrived, her taxi having been held up in the traffic building up outside because of the crowd of people gathering around the doorway, the news of the marriage having leaked out somehow. James' agent had probably considered it good publicity, even if James didn't.

She only had time to give her brother and Sheri a quick kiss on the cheek before they had to go in and start the ceremony. She felt quite emotional during the marriage, much more emotional than when she had left the house to move into her flat. After all, James was no longer just her brother, his first duty must always lie with his wife from now on, and much as she herself loved Sheri and welcomed her into the family she couldn't help crying.

She went out with the other selected guests to see them off to the reception, almost getting crushed in the rush of the fans to get a look at their idol and the celebrated model he had just married. She was jostled and knocked about until she thought she was going to fall over and be crushed underfoot.

'Just hang on to me, Kate,' rasped a familiar voice very close to her ear, and she felt a firm grip on her upper arm.

'And for God's sake stop crying! Stop making a damned fool of yourself!'

Her tears stopped instantly and she turned to face Damien Savage. God, how handsome he looked, dressed completely in white, the jacket to his suit fitting tautly across his powerful shoulders, his tanned skin making him look slightly foreign—and very exciting. She always noticed this about him, the way he appeared exciting, even angry as he was now.

'Damien,' she murmured softly, not sure whether she was glad to see him or not. She had wanted to see him quite desperately a couple of times in the last month, but to be suddenly confronted with him like this had thrown her completely off balance. He must have been at the wedding all the time and she hadn't even realised. He looked so tall and sophisticated standing there, so completely the man in control. 'I didn't know you were here,' she said lamely.

'I'm not surprised,' he returned dryly, dragging her along with him, uncaring of the people gaping at him as he became recognised. 'You appeared to have eyes for no one but the bridegroom—and his bride, of course.'

They had reached his car parked in a quiet side-street, its sleek lines drawing almost as much attention as its owner. He thrust her inside before coming round to get in behind the steering-wheel, slamming the car into gear and accelerating away from the curious faces watching them through the smoky windows.

'I wasn't even sure you would be at the wedding at all, let alone act as one of the witnesses.' He gave her a hard look. 'What are you, a masochist?'

'No.' She cleared her throat, loving the tangy smell of his aftershave. She felt happy to be with him and apprehensive at the same time, but most of all she felt aware of him as completely male, sensual and dominant. 'James asked me and I——'

'You agreed!' he finished scathingly, those green eyes of his raking over her mercilessly. 'How could you do that to yourself? Don't you have any pride?'

'I have plenty, but I——'

'Didn't it bother you that you should have been the bride?' he cut in. 'Didn't you feel anything!'

Damn James and his infernal lie! Damien still thought she had been going to marry James. 'You know I felt something, you saw me crying.'

'Mm,' he said unfeelingly. 'It must be heartbreaking to see all that lovely money going to another woman. I must say I didn't expect James to react quite so drastically.'

Kate sighed. 'What do you mean now?'

'Tell me,' he ignored her question, 'does Sheri know James asked her to marry him on the rebound?'

She gasped. 'He did no such thing! Surely you could see how happy they were just now? As any normal newly married couple should be.'

'Oh sure, they looked happy enough. I think James must have finally got you out of his system. What happened after I left, did he say to hell with the marriage and take you anyway?'

'No doubt that's what you would have done?'

'Sure I would. Why pay the price of a wedding ring for something that everyone else seems to be getting for nothing? Besides, I can't think of any other way of getting you out of the system.'

'Well, he didn't!' she said crossly.

'More fool him,' Damien muttered. 'I guess he just couldn't take the fact that you'd been with me.'

'But I hadn't!'

'I'm sure he didn't believe that.'

'Why shouldn't he? I had no reason to lie.'

He gave a sardonic smile. 'Only a wedding ring. Tell me, Kate, why did you suddenly decide a wedding ring was so important?'

'I've always considered it important,' she told him with a sigh, sick of his opinion of her but knowing of no way to change it.

He came round to open her door for her, handing his car keys to the doorman before guiding her into the hotel. James and Sheri were waiting to greet them as they came into the reception room and they were far from being the first to arrive. James' face darkened as they came into the room together.

'Where have you been?' he demanded of Kate. 'Tony was supposed to bring you here. He's been looking everywhere for you.'

'Damien insisted on bringing me.'

James looked at the other man sharply as if noticing him for the first time, although Kate felt sure he had noticed her companion long before this. 'Damien,' he nodded curtly.

Damien gave his hand a firm shake, smiling unconcernedly in the face of the other man's displeasure. 'I found her without your help,' he remarked quietly.

'So I see,' James snapped, and turned from him impatiently. 'Now look, Kate, I want you to steer clear of my mother. She's on the warpath,' he warned her. 'She has her acid look on today. She's already remarked on the garishness of my friends. She could give you a hard time of it if she decided to dig her claws into you.'

'Kate's with me, James,' Damien told him arrogantly. 'I think I can safeguard her from your mother.'

Unwillingly James smiled. 'You don't know my mother!'

'I don't need to. Just leave her to me.' He took a firm grip of Kate's arm again. 'We'd better move in and let your other guests come and say hello. Ready, Kate?'

'Oh yes—ready.' She hugged James and kissed Sheri on the cheek. 'I'm going to like having you for a sister,' she whispered.

'Thank you.' Sheri smiled tremulously, looking beautiful, as all brides do.

'Why doesn't James' mother like you?' Damien asked once they both had a drink in their hand.

Kate hesitated. 'Oh, she—well, she just doesn't.'

'I suppose I can guess the reason.'

She could imagine! 'What did you mean when you told James you found me without his help?' That statement had been puzzling her somewhat.

He shrugged, looking round at the other guests as he sipped his drink. 'Well, I have, haven't I?'

'Yes, but did you—did you want to find me?'

'I told you I wanted you and would do anything to get you.' He turned to look at her now. 'James didn't seem too willing to tell me where you're living now. But I knew you would turn up some time, your sort always do.'

'My sort?' She frowned.

'Mm. I knew you'd soon be on the lookout for another rich boy-friend. I just had to make sure I was about when it happened.'

'Why, you——'

'Ah, Katherine, my dear.' A tall woman with perfectly coiffured grey hair came up to them, her grey eyes so like her son's, as hard as granite at the moment, her expression one of frosty disdain. 'I thought I would find you here to-day.'

'Yes.' Kate felt overawed as she usually did when in the company of James' mother. 'The wedding was very lovely, wasn't it?'

'Very,' Louise St Just agreed. 'And I'm so glad James chose a sensible girl. I didn't approve of the two of you living together as you were. At least now you've had to move out—even if James is still supporting you financially.'

'He doesn't support me!' James hadn't been joking when he had said his mother was in a bitchy mood, but Kate found it very embarrassing that Damien had to witness this.

She had felt him stiffen when Louise came over to them, and now he looked thunderous. But she personally couldn't wholly blame Louise for her hard, embittered attitude towards her. It couldn't be easy to be suddenly confronted with her husband's child by another woman, especially as James didn't share her resentful attitude.

Kate had had these sort of arguments with Louise St Just many times in the last four years, and although she didn't like it, she could understand it. But not in front of Damien! So far Louise hadn't got round to the insulting names she usually resorted to, and she hadn't let it out about her being Richard St Just's illegitimate child, but knowing her of old she knew it wouldn't be long before she did.

'You know the reason for the allowance,' she retorted quietly, ever conscious of Damien's keen glance.

'Oh yes, I know. I've always known—how could I not with James thrusting it down my throat all the time? And I thought it quite disgusting that you should act as a witness to my son's wedding. I wouldn't have thought you capable of recognising that there was such a thing as marriage.'

Goodness, she was in good form today! 'I believe in marriage, Mrs St Just. It just isn't possible for some people.' Her mother, Angela Stevens, and Richard St Just had met when her mother had become his temporary secretary during his own secretary's illness. It had been instant attraction for both of them, although because of Richard's marriage they had both fought against it.

But their romance had been inevitable, only ending after a few months' duration because his wife found out about their illicit love affair and demanded an end to it. Richard had asked for a divorce but had been firmly denied it, his wife pointing out that his reputation wouldn't stand it.

Kate could imagine it had been a traumatic time for her mother, being only twenty to Richard's already forty years. But it had been made all the worse by Louise St Just's spiteful attitude to the younger girl, even going so far as to visit her and tell her what a mess she was making of her husband's life. Her mother had been impressionable and shy, only her overwhelming love for the sophisticated and distinguished Richard causing her to have the one moral lapse of her life. She had paid dearly for that moral lapse, the birth of her child, Kate, a child completely unknown to the father as her mother had already opted out of his life.

No matter what Louise St Just might have thought of the younger girl her mother had not been the sort of girl to use the leverage of her expected baby to force him into leaving his wife and son. And so she had quietly disappeared from his life and he had never heard from her again, until her death, when she had left the care of their child to him.

But even now, all these years later, Louise St Just couldn't forgive and forget, taking out her anger and humiliation on the child of that liaison. Kate was used to it now, but she couldn't allow this to happen in front of Damien.

'No,' Louise agreed. 'Your sort seem to have a penchant for other women's husbands. I hope James is sensible and keeps you out of his life in future.'

'I would think that's highly possible, Mrs St Just,' Damien spoke for the first time. 'If you hadn't yet noticed, Kate is here with me.'

Grey eyes swept over his relaxed arrogance, the sneer left her face and a charming smile lit up her beautiful but ageing face. 'Mr Savage,' she purred. 'How nice to meet you! James has talked a lot about you.'

'Really?' he returned dryly.

'Yes, really. I'm afraid you'll have to excuse Katherine and me, we're old adversaries. If you know anything about my family at all you'll realise why.'

'I guess so. But like I told you, Kate is with me now,' he told her hardly. 'James can take care of his wife in future, I'm taking care of Kate.'

Louise gave Kate a scathing look. 'You'll never change, will you—you and Angela, both with the morals of an alley-cat!'

Kate saw red, a high flush to her cheeks. 'Now that's enough!' Her own insults she would take but not ones against her mother.

'I couldn't agree more,' Damien interrupted softly, too softly, his gaze rapier-sharp. 'I think you would be wise to remove yourself from our company, Mrs St Just. After all, you might become tainted by our lax morals.'

Louise's mouth tightened at his deliberate snub. 'Perhaps you're right,' she nodded haughtily. 'Good afternoon.'

Damien watched her go, his face grim. 'Not a pleasant woman,' he remarked coldly. 'And she obviously hates your guts. I suppose that's because you enslaved her precious son. Mothers are always like that over their only children.'

Kate could have laughed at the irony of that statement; it was because James *wasn't* an only child that his mother was so embittered. She couldn't bear sharing his affections with his half-sister, she had hated her mother and the hate had passed on to Kate.

'Is your mother the same?' she couldn't resist asking.

He gave a slight smile. 'My mother's the opposite. She's openly admitted that she'll laugh herself silly if some poor female gets me hooked.'

'*Poor* female?'

'Mm,' he grinned openly now. 'The Savage men are known for their—let's call it rakish behaviour. We're equally well known for being possessive as hell when we do fall in love, and we all fall in the end. I'm just taking longer to do it than most, which doesn't please my mother. She swears I'm doing it on purpose because I know she wants grandchildren, as an only child I'm thwarting her plans somewhat.'

'Then why haven't you married?'

'I'll marry when I'm good and ready, not to suit someone

else. I've known a lot of women and loved none of them. I'm beginning to wonder if the woman I could love has been born yet. There has to be more to love than sexual need.'

Oh, there was, Kate had found that out since she had realised she loved him. Sometimes love happened suddenly and unexpectedly, or so she believed; it had for her anyway. Initial hostility, fear even, had turned to blinding love. And he was right, she wanted him in the fullest sense of the word, but she also enjoyed just being with him. But he believed her to be promiscuous, hardly the sort of girl he would ever fall in love with.

'I suppose we'll have to mingle a bit,' he muttered tersely. 'But don't go wandering off. I'm taking you home once Sheri and James have left. We have a lot to talk about, like when are you going to move in with me?'

CHAPTER SIX

KATE shook her head firmly. 'I'm not moving in with anyone. I've just got my freedom from one——'

'Lover,' he supplied harshly.

'Man,' she finished, ignoring his interruption. 'I'm not going to give that up to pander to another man's whims and demands. James was unbearably bossy and I'm sure you would be even worse than him.' Much worse, because she would want him as her lover, and once that happened she would be his slave for life.

Damien gave her an impatient look. 'We'll discuss that later.'

'I'm not going to your apartment again,' she stated adamantly.

'I know you're not,' he agreed instantly. 'We're going to yours. I want to know where you're living. As the only other person who seems to have that information James is singularly unco-operative. He refused point blank to tell me where you were when I asked him.'

'Probably because he realises, as I do, that your only interest in me is sexual. You've made no secret of that.'

'So what? James can't be allowed to keep you *and* have Sheri as his wife. Does he really pay you an allowance?' he threw the question at her, reminding her of his behaviour the first time they had met.

'Yes,' she answered truthfully.

'And pay for your apartment?'

'Yes.'

His face darkened. 'That will have to stop. I'm not having you kept by anyone but me. Oh, hell!' He began to

99

scowl again. 'Here comes Diana Hall. Try not to get bitchy with each other this time.'

Diana Hall was indeed approaching them, her blue eyes set very determinedly on Damien. Kate held her head high. 'I wouldn't give you the satisfaction.'

'That isn't the sort of satisfaction I want from you.' He gave a husky laugh at her flaming cheeks. 'Now, now, behave yourself,' he taunted as her anger grew.

Kate clamped her lips together to stop her angry retort. She wouldn't let him see how easily he could annoy her. Diana Hall had reached them by now, threading her hand through the crook of Damien's arm and leaning intimately against his side. The sight of the other girl drooling all over him only sickened Kate and she knew she had to get away before she made a fool of herself and said something she would regret.

'I'm just going to see Sheri and James,' she interrupted Damien's throaty chuckle at something the other girl had whispered in his ear.

Diana stopped giggling long enough to give her a scathing glance. 'Can't you even leave them alone on their wedding day?' she scorned. 'Really, Kate, couldn't you at least wait until they get back from their honeymoon?'

Kate held on to her temper with difficulty. This girl's taunts had come too soon after Louise St Just's vitriolic tongue. 'I said James *and* Sheri, Diana,' she said in a controlled voice. 'If you'll both excuse me . . .'

She didn't get very far before she felt a firm grip on her arm, and she turned resignedly to face Damien. Diana Hall was watching them curiously and she could see several other people looking their way.

'Just where do you think you're going?' he asked grimly, concerned only with her.

She sighed. 'I already told you that, I'm going to see James and Sheri.'

'Do you have to? Everyone's already commenting on you being here at all without that.'

She wrenched out of his grasp, her brown eyes glaring at him angrily. 'I'm not answerable to you or anyone else for my actions. I shall see who I want *when* I want.'

'Okay, okay, maybe I don't have any say in that—yet. But I'm still taking you home, so don't try a disappearing act on me. I can be quite brutal when thwarted,' he warned her, his eyes narrowed.

'I can imagine!'

'Just remember it.'

'Oh, I will. Have fun with your little—friend,' she scorned. 'I'm sure she'll keep you well entertained until I get back.'

'Jealous, Kate?' he taunted.

Very, but she wasn't going to tell him that. 'Not in the least. I wouldn't waste my time on such a useless emotion. Look, I have to see James and Sheri, they'll be leaving in a moment.'

'All right.' His green eyes were grim. 'But don't try and leave without me.'

With a defiant flick of her head she left him to go up to the room her brother and Sheri were using to change. It had been provided by the hotel as part of the service and Kate wanted to go up and say a private goodbye there. She couldn't wish them the luck she wanted to in front of all the other guests.

She went to knock on the door, hesitating slightly as she heard Sheri giggling. All sound was cut off at the sound of her knock and she blushed at her stupidity. This was the first time the happy couple had been alone since they became man and wife, and they certainly wouldn't want her bursting in on their privacy.

She was just turning away when a red-faced James opened the door. 'Kate!' he grinned his relief at its being here. 'I thought it was one of the hotel staff. Come on in.'

She shied away from actually going into the room; she had obviously picked the wrong time to come up here. 'I can see you later, James, when you get downstairs.'

'Don't be ridiculous! Get in here.'

'No, I——'

Sheri came to the door. 'Will you come in, Kate, and stop trying to be polite.' She smiled. 'James has waited this long for me, I'm sure he can wait until we reach Venice. Come *on*, Kate.'

She did as she was told, admiring Sheri's clinging scarlet dress that she had chosen to wear for her flight. 'You look beautiful, Sheri,' she blinked away the tears that seemed to have gathered in her eyes again. 'You looked lovely at the wedding too.'

'Thank you. You're looking exceptionally beautiful yourself today.'

James scowled at the two of them as he fastened the buttons to his navy shirt, the jacket to his white suit the only thing he needed to put on now to complete his change of clothing. 'It's no good the two of you carrying on like this, I haven't forgotten about Damien Savage and I'm not likely to. What were you doing, turning up here with him?'

'Well, I——'

He didn't wait for her to finish. 'I didn't even know he'd been invited to the actual wedding. I don't remember inviting him.'

'I did that,' put in Sheri. 'He was at Ben's party last week and I—I thought it only polite to ask him. After all, you are going to be working for him when we get back from the honeymoon and I——' she trailed off, looking appealingly at her new husband. 'I'm sorry, James.'

The scowl left his face. 'Hey, no need to get upset, it's all right.' He gave her an encouraging smile. 'I just wish I'd known, that's all.'

Kate shrugged. 'What difference would that have made? We would still have met.'

'Met, yes. But I could have got Sheri's brother to keep a better eye on you.'

Sheri gave a scoffing laugh. 'You think Tony would be much protection against Damien?'

'Well ... perhaps not,' he allowed.

'Definitely not,' she corrected. 'I've seen Damien in action and my kid brother wouldn't stand a chance. Damien's arrogance would frighten the life out of him.'

'Mm,' Kate agreed. 'Even your mother was slightly over-awed, James.'

'Oh, lord!' he looked worried. 'She spoke to you, then?'

'Oh yes. Still, it wasn't too bad,' she lied. 'I only came up here to say my goodbyes. I don't want to keep you.'

'You aren't keeping us—and stop trying to change the subject. My mother was very objectionable, I can tell that at a glance.'

'She was,' Kate agreed. 'But she didn't give us away, actually she just made things sound worse than they are.'

'And where's Damien now?'

'He's downstairs, waiting to take me home.'

'You aren't going home with him!' James exclaimed, outraged. 'Look what happened the last time you were alone with him.'

'*Nearly* happened, James.'

'Okay, nearly happened. God, I deliberately didn't tell him where you were living now, and he just calmly turns up here and walks off with you. You aren't strong enough to refuse his brand of seduction, and you certainly aren't going home with him.'

'James!' His wife looked shocked. 'Kate's an adult, and you can't tell her who she can or can't meet.'

Kate sighed, 'He's always done it.'

'Then it's high time he stopped. You can't rule her life

for ever, James. Kate has to find out for herself about the wolves of this world, like I did. The only trouble is that I'm married to one,' she finished teasingly.

James laughed. 'Since meeting you I'm a reformed character.'

'So maybe our Kate will reform Damien, who knows?'

'I do,' he said firmly. 'Damien's untamable.'

'James, you said you deliberately didn't tell him where I was living,' Kate said slowly. 'Did he ask?'

He nodded. 'A couple of times. I refused to tell him.'

It seemed to Kate quite a break-through for someone who said they never chased women. And it was a break-through she wanted to follow up. 'Well, he's going to find out now, because he wants to take me home, and I want him to.'

'But you can't——'

'I can, James,' she declared firmly. 'And I'm going to.' She moved towards the door. 'I'll leave you two to finish getting ready. You can't keep your guests waiting much longer.'

'Kate, you——'

'That's fine,' Sheri cut in, giving Kate a glowing smile. 'And while we're on our honeymoon I'll try and convince this handsome hunk of a brother of yours that you're a big girl now.'

'I know she's a big girl now, *that's* why I'm worried. And don't try telling me she can take care of herself because I know for a fact that she can't, not where Damien's concerned anyway—can you, Kate?'

She felt her cheeks suffuse with colour. 'It's not for want of trying.'

'I know that, love,' he said gently. 'So you'll be careful?'

'If I can't be good, hmm?' she joked.

Now it was his turn to look uncomfortable. 'Now you know I didn't mean that—yes, I did! You be damned careful.'

'I'm sure to remember to be that, James. How can I be anything else when I think of my own entrance into the world? I wouldn't wish illegitimacy on anyone. Now I'm not going to discuss Damien with you any more,' she smiled brightly. 'I only came to say my goodbyes, and I've said them already.'

'I'll see you to the door.' James slipped on his jacket.

Actually he came out into the corridor with her, looking down at her searchingly. Kate tried her best to look happy, but in truth she felt tearful again. James was all the family she had and she was going to miss him during the next few weeks.

She stood on tiptoe to kiss his cheek. 'Take care, James. And be happy.'

'Thanks, Kate,' he said gruffly. 'And please be careful of Damien. I don't want to come back and find you've become his latest woman.'

She laughed huskily. 'Do you think that's likely?'

'I think it's very likely when I'm not here to look after you.'

'I'll try to behave until you get back.'

'I wish there were some way I could—well, that I could——'

Kate shook her head. 'There's no way you can go on honeymoon with Sheri *and* stay here with me. I'll still be here when you get back.'

'But things will never be the same. I've realised the last few weeks just how much I'm going to miss you, you've lived with me for so long now I got used to your being around.'

'And it showed,' she told him dryly. 'You were really beginning to take me for granted, James—admit it.'

'I suppose I was. But I—I liked having you about.'

'I'll still be about, just living in my own flat. You can visit me often.'

'Mm, I will. In fact, I'll be over to see you the day we

get back. I'll call you this evening when we reach Venice.'

Kate looked at him sharply. 'What's that for? To let me know you've arrived safely, or to check that I'm at home alone?'

'Both,' he answered without hesitation.

She had to laugh at his honesty. 'I'll see you when you get back. Have fun!' She reached up and kissed him again. 'Go on, back you go to Sheri before I disgrace myself and start crying again.'

'All right. But you take care of yourself.'

'I will.' She opened the door and gently pushed him back into the room. 'I love you and I want you to be happy.'

'Thanks, Kate.'

She softly closed the door and turned away, making a conscious effort to pull herself together. She came face to face with Damien. 'Oh . . .' she said weakly.

'Yes, oh.' His look was contemptuous. 'I'll say this for you, Kate, you really have style. James has just got himself married, his bride is waiting for him on the other side of that door, and you're out here kissing him and making arrangements to meet him when he gets back from his honeymoon. I'll give you full marks for sheer nerve!'

Her eyes darkened with distress. 'It wasn't like that——'

'It damn well was! I've been out here for quite some time and I heard it all. It's Sheri I feel sorry for. And what I'm learning about you I don't like.'

'What you're learning isn't strictly me.' She sighed. 'You're just reading what you want to in what I say, seeing what you want to see.'

'I don't think there's any other way to see it. Let's get out of here,' he added, suddenly impatient. 'Weddings have never been on my list of pleasurable activities. I avoid them where possible.'

'So I've noticed.'

'Mm—well, are you ready to go now? You've arranged

to meet James, he's going to call you this evening, so there can't be much else you want to do here.'

'He'll expect to see me when they come down.'

Damien grasped her arm and led her purposefully towards one of the exits. 'Then he can damn well expect,' he declared grimly, indicating for his car to be brought round to the front of the hotel. 'I don't share my women with anyone!'

Kate gasped as he thrust her inside the car and angrily walked round to get in beside her. 'I'm not one of your women!' she told him adamantly.

'But you're going to be. And for the time I'm in your life I'm going to be the only one. Get that?'

'Oh, don't start that again. I don't want to be your mistress and I'm not moving in with you.'

'You'll do as you're told!' His gaze remained fiercely on the road in front of him. 'What's your address?'

'Don't you dare talk to me like that! You don't *own* me.'

'No, but I'm going to. You have a lesson to learn about human relationships, and I'm going to teach it to you. James is married now and I think you should leave him alone. He's a man, and he won't make the first move to finish things between the two of you—you'll have to do that. You can start tonight by not answering his call.'

'I will not! He'll wonder what's happened to me. He'll worry,' she added.

'If you don't answer his call he'll know what's happened to you, you'll be with me. And he should have better things to do than worry about his mistress on his wedding night. I'm surprised Sheri allows things between you to go on still, she's never appeared to me to be the complaisant sort.' His expression hardened as he looked at her. 'Don't you feel in the least guilty about what you're doing to her?'

'Are you trying to find some good in me somewhere?' she scorned hotly. 'Because the way you twist things I doubt you'll find anything.'

'Don't blame your inadequacies on my twisted mind. Now, your address?'

Reluctantly Kate told him. It wasn't easy to defy him, he was so forceful. And so very attractive. The last few weeks had done nothing to dull her attraction to him, in fact she found him even more fascinating. And yet, in a way, he also frightened her. How could she both love and fear him at the same time? With startling clarity she realised that the two emotions were deeply connected. She loved Damien and yet feared the power that gave him over her.

It wasn't the sort of love she had wanted to feel for any man, sure that this was a similar emotion to the one her mother must have felt for Richard St Just. And look what had happened to her!

Kate had wanted the secure sort of love, the dull everyday sort of love that most of her school friends had always talked about, the sort of love their parents had for each other. She didn't want to be in love with the elusive Damien Savage, ravaged by emotions that could eventually tear her apart.

She had always looked down on the feelings her mother must have felt for her lover, always thought her mother should have had more will-power than to fall in love with a married man. But now she knew how her mother must have felt for this dynamic man, the temptation it must have been to sacrifice all her principles for one night in his arms. But she wasn't going to fall into the same trap, not for Damien or any other man!

The flat was in chaos when she let them in a few moments later. Josie came bursting out of the bedroom, frantically pulling rollers out of her hair. 'Oh, Kate,' she cried, 'everything's gone wrong! My hair wouldn't dry, I smudged my nail-varnish, and somehow my dress has got all creased along the bottom. I'll never be ready!'

'Calm down, Josie,' Kate said soothingly. 'I thought you were the one who was all organised.'

'So did I,' Josie groaned.

'Okay, well just calm yourself. You brush out your hair and re-do your nails, and I'll go and iron your dress. It's that stupid wardrobe, of course, it simply isn't tall enough.'

Josie began to look less panic-stricken. 'Oh, thanks, Kate. You're a love!'

Kate removed the jacket to her suit, pinning back her own hair with a wooden slide. 'I won't be two minutes,' she promised.

'Kate?'

She looked up with a start at the sound of that soft drawl and Josie looked no less surprised. Damien was watching the two of them through narrowed green eyes and Kate couldn't imagine how she had ever forgotten he was here. Probably because she had been trying to.

'Oh, Damien. Look, I—I won't be a minute. Josie has to go out in a couple of minutes and—well, as you see, she isn't ready.' She moved her shoulders helplessly.

'Yes, I can see,' he drawled. 'I just wondered who Josie was.'

'Josie's my flatmate,' she told him shortly. 'Josie, this is Damien Savage. Damien, Josie Walker.'

He put out his hand politely. 'Nice to meet you, Josie.' He looked down at her slender hand. 'And your nail-varnish looks fine to me.'

Josie was obviously bowled over by his charm, for the moment forgetting her need for speed, her face lighting up with excitement as she looked at him. 'Gosh, Damien Savage! It's very exciting sharing with Kate, I'm getting to meet a lot of famous people.'

Damien's eyes clearly mocked as he turned to look at Kate. 'I'm sure you do, Josie, I'm sure you do. Kate's a popular girl.'

'Yes. She——'

'I'm just going to iron your dress, Josie,' Kate interrupted. 'I should get your hair done or you'll be late.'

'Goodness, yes! Excuse me, Mr Savage.'

'Go right ahead. And please, call me Damien.' He settled himself down in an armchair. 'I have a feeling you'll be seeing me here quite a lot in future.'

Within ten minutes Josie had left the flat in a whirlwind of perfume and glossy black curls. She had glowed as Damien complimented her on her appearance, finally dashing out of the flat at the sound of the doorbell.

Damien smiled his amusement. 'I like your friend, she's cute.'

'I'll tell her you said so,' Kate snapped. 'I'm sure she'll be overjoyed.'

His mouth tightened. 'I'm just wondering where she fits into things. Does James have himself a harem going here? Is Josie another one of his women?'

Kate could have laughed at his outrageousness. 'You're really something! You say you like Josie and then in the next breath you insult her.'

'Well, is she?'

'Josie just happens to be the girl I share this flat with, nothing else. She has an important date this evening with her boss. She wanted to look her best for him.'

'If he has any sense he'll marry her. There aren't many fresh-faced kids like her about any more.'

'I'm sure Paul feels the same way,' she told him dryly. 'Or at least he will by the end of the evening.'

'She's out to get him, I gather?'

She looked annoyed. 'Do you always have to mock everything? Josie happens to love Paul, and that's the only reason she would like to marry him.'

'Like I said, she's a cute kid. Why can't you be more like her?'

'I am like her, you just don't want to see it.'

'Oh, but I do. There's nothing I would like better than to find you're as innocent as you pretend to be, if that were the case I'd probably lose interest. I don't prey on innocents. But you're something else completely, you like to *play* at being innocent. I guess I'm getting a little tired of that game now. I've come clean with you, I've admitted that I still want you like hell—do you need to wring any more admissions from me? What else does it take to get you to give in?'

Kate turned away from the desire in his eyes, looked away from the warmth in his devilish green eyes for her. He was too sophisticated, too lethal for her peace of mind. 'I don't give in to anyone,' she told him quietly.

Damien stood up, his movements impatient. 'Look, you move in with James——'

'That was purely innocent. I had my own room,' she insisted. 'And James never entered it.'

'Okay, okay,' he silenced her abruptly. 'But if you moved in with him what's to stop you moving in with me?'

She gave a harsh laugh. 'I think you know the answer to that.'

'What the hell are you scared of?' Damien demanded angrily. 'Has some man frightened you in the past, forced you into some sort of situation you didn't want to be in? Why the aversion to men? I'm sure it must be a recent acquisition.'

Kate shook her head. 'You're wrong. It isn't recent at all. I learnt at an early age of the immorality of men. Do you have any idea what your sort of relationships lead to, the heartache it can cause?'

'You would know the score from the beginning, that it would never lead to the love and marriage bit.' His eyes narrowed as he looked at her.

She gave him a pitying look. 'And you think that knowledge prevents those feelings developing?' She shook her head. 'If you think that then you don't know women as well as you think you do. We don't think with our bodies but

with our hearts. And our heart has to be involved to a
certain degree for a physical relationship to take place—at
least, mine does.'

'You want me too, Kate, so stop blinding yourself with
words. If you want to move in with me for a few weeks, no
strings attached, then I'm agreeable to that. I wouldn't ask
anything of you.'

The offer was so tempting, but she knew it wouldn't
work, that she wouldn't be able to trust herself. And sooner
or later Damien would want to share her bed. 'You wouldn't
need to,' she admitted. 'I think you know why.'

'Because you want me!' he said angrily. 'I don't know
what else I can offer you, what else you want of me.' His
face had darkened ominously with his anger. 'I don't aim
to marry anyone just to get a body I desire.'

'That's all it is to you, all it can ever be to you!' Kate
snapped. 'Have you ever thought what could happen from
such an alliance? Did it ever occur to you that an unwanted
child could be born through your *desire*?'

'There are ways of preventing such things,' he scorned.

'And when they fail?' she asked shrilly, the subject too
dear to her own heart for her to remain objective about it.
'It isn't you or I that would suffer, it would be the child. I
know—my mother wasn't married to my father. I haven't
forgotten what it was like at school, or how my stepfather
thrust that knowledge down both my mother's and my
throat at every opportunity. Now do you realise why I
won't ever enter into an affair, why you'll never get me to
live with you? I wouldn't wish my childhood on anyone!'

'Oh, God!' Damien groaned, moving closer to her.
'Come here, Kate. This seems to be the only way I have of
reaching you.' He bent his head to claim her lips in a kiss
that reduced all her arguments to nothing.

He was right: this was the only way they communicated,
when words no longer seemed to matter between them.
Her mouth moved below his in passionate longing, her

arms up about his neck as she strained him closer to her.

He used the whole of his experience to inflame her, her body against his, the hard length of his thighs firmly imprinted against hers. The heavy rise and fall of his chest made her aware of his own heightened senses, the pounding of his heart as fast as her own.

Damien teased her lips apart to better claim her sweetness, his hands sure and firm as they moved across her back. One hand moved round to cup her breast, her whole body sensitive to his touch. And her own hands weren't idle, smoothing the muscled skin of his back beneath his jacket.

'Oh, Kate,' he sighed against her lips. 'You can be so sweet. Why do you have to fight me?'

'I already told you that.' She rested her forehead on his chin. 'I won't let that happen to me.'

'I wouldn't let it, honey,' he said gently.

'*I* wasn't planned, Damien.' She shook her head. 'I'm sorry, but you'll have to find someone else for that sort of fun.'

He was touching her hair with strong tanned hands, smoothing the silken tresses down her back. 'And if I don't want anyone else?'

'Then I'm sorry.'

'No, you're not. I think you enjoy torturing me. Am I being paid back for the mistake your father made?'

He thwarted all her efforts to move out of his arms. 'Let me go, Damien! How can you say such things to me? I'm not paying anyone back for anything.'

Damien held her firmly against him. 'Oh yes, you are, honey. You like to give the come-on and then say no. Your hair,' he murmured softly. 'Do you always wear it loose now?'

'Not always, no,' she answered resentfully. 'I—It——'

'You know I prefer it loose. You wear it like this to please me.'

This time she did wrench out of his arms, moving a safe distance away from him, as safe as she could be when still in the same room as him. Her anger was all the stronger because he was right. He was always right about her. Always.

'I wear it like this to please myself, no one else.'

'You're lying. You told me you didn't like it loose.'

'Do you have to remember everything I've said so clearly?' she snapped. 'Someone told me it suited me like this.'

'That's right—I did.'

'No, not you.'

Those green eyes darkened and his lips snapped together angrily. 'Who else have you been out with the last couple of months?'

'Why should I tell you that? It has nothing to do with you, nothing!'

'All right, that's it! I've had it with you. I'll grovel to no woman. I want you, but I'm not going to beg you for anything.' Damien's face was contorted with rage. 'Maybe one day I'll meet someone I feel that strongly about, but it won't be made through blackmail!'

'Oh, but I'm not——'

'Yes, you damn well are!' he ground out. 'Maybe I'll see you around—but I wouldn't count on it. I intend avoiding you at every opportunity.'

'Damien, I'm sorry. I——'

'Don't add insult to injury! Just get your claws into some other poor guy who'll find your elusiveness entertaining. I've gone past that stage with you now.' He walked over to the door. 'Way past. If I don't get out of here I'm going to do something we'll both regret.'

The whole room seemed to shake as he slammed the door after him. Kate sank weakly into a chair, the trauma of the last few hours almost too much for her. So much had happened today, not least of all Louise St Just's unwarranted attack on her. James would have been furious if he had known the extent of his mother's nastiness.

But Damien walking out on her in that way had just about finished her off. But what else could she expect? The situation between them was explosive, positively lethal. Where would it all end, if it hadn't already ended? She must make sure that this was the end, before things got out of hand. If they hadn't already!

She was still sitting in the chair when Josie returned at midnight, James' telephone call previously the only interruption into her loneliness. Josie came quietly into the room and switched on the small side-lamps. She looked taken aback as she spotted Kate. 'I thought you would either be out or fast asleep in bed.' She slipped off her coat and came to sit down.

'I must have fallen asleep,' Kate lied, having been staring thoughtfully into the darkness for the last few hours since James' call.

Josie looked at her concernedly. 'Have you eaten?'

'I wasn't hungry,' she said dully.

'Weddings are always an anti-climax, aren't they,' Josie chattered on. 'I always feel thoroughly deflated.'

Kate summoned up a smile. 'Never mind, it'll be your turn soon. How did your evening go, by the way? As if I need to ask!' Josie was glowing and it didn't need two guesses why.

'The evening was—fantastic. He's taking me out for a picnic tomorrow.'

'That should be nice.'

'And you—how did your evening go?'

Kate looked away. 'I've been home all evening.'

'Oh, did Mr Savage have to leave?'

'Yes,' she answered shortly.

'Are you seeing him again? He's really lovely looking,' Josie enthused.

Kate shook her head. 'I won't be seeing him again. I'm

sure of it.' And she didn't know if she was pleased or sad about it. Sad, she thought, although things had become too strained between them. But it was over now, over! If it had ever really begun.

CHAPTER SEVEN

'GOD, I'm tired!' James slumped down into an armchair. 'Sorry I'm so late, but Damien is working like a demon—and expects everyone else to do the same.'

The smile faded from Kate's lips at the mention of Damien. She tried to think of him as little as possible, but just occasionally someone mentioned him casually and the old heartache started up again. But this time she wouldn't let it. She had Alan now, and she wouldn't let thoughts of Damien ruin that for her.

It was ten weeks since she had last seen him, and they were well into production with the film, hence James' moans and groans. During that time she had met Alan Reed, a tall, well-built man of moderate good looks and a generous nature. Kate had liked him from the first and had gladly accepted his invitation to the theatre. The two of them had met at a party Josie had insisted on taking her to, and fortunately he had no connection with acting. She felt she needed a break from that type.

'You aren't late, James. Alan hasn't arrived yet.'

'It's pretty decent of him to offer me a lift home.'

'Well, he hasn't exactly done that yet,' she laughed. 'But as we're going to your party it seems only fair we should take you with us.'

'Damned car, breaking down like that,' he scowled. 'I could have got a taxi, I suppose, but——'

'It isn't necessary,' she interrupted. 'Not when we're going to your place anyway.' She handed him a coffee.

'Thanks.' He drank some of it thirstily. 'I've never worked as hard as I have this past few weeks. Damien's insatiable when it comes to work.'

117

'That's how he got to be the best,' she said stiffly, back to the subject she had hoped to avoid. 'He's a perfectionist.'

'But this isn't normal—everyone's complaining.'

'Never mind,' she smiled. 'You can all air your grievances together tonight and then go back to work tomorrow with fresh minds.'

'Hardly.' He visibly started to relax, the lines of tension starting to leave his mouth. 'I don't think Damien would appreciate the criticism, and he's hell to work for already without that.'

Kate looked at him sharply, a feeling of dread starting to invade her body. 'Damien is going to be there tonight?'

'We could hardly not invite him, everyone else to do with the film is coming.'

'Matt Strange too?'

'Mm,' James grimaced. 'He's turning out to be just as obnoxious as I always thought he was. And he's always surrounded by girls,' he added with disgust.

'Jealous?' she teased.

'No. I'm past the stage where I have to have girls clinging to me all day to prove how clever and handsome I am. Besides,' he grinned, 'Sheri wouldn't like it.'

That marriage agreed with her brother was obvious; he and Sheri were positively glowing with love for each other when they returned from their honeymoon.

'You're right,' she agreed, 'she wouldn't.'

'No Josie tonight?'

'She has a dinner date with Paul.'

'Getting serious, isn't it?' he frowned.

'Yes, I think so.' She knew that the couple had already started talking of marriage.

James sighed. 'That's all we need! Well, if Josie moves out you're coming back home. I don't like your living here.'

'You aren't going to like what I did today any better,' she told him guiltily. 'I enrolled into a secretarial course.'

'You did what!' His cup landed in the saucer with a clatter.

'Now don't get annoyed, James,' she calmed him. 'I've tried to find a job the last few weeks, with no success. The only way to get a job nowadays is to have some sort of training behind you, and I don't have any.'

'But a secretarial course!'

Kate laughed at his undisguised disgust. 'There's nothing wrong with being a secretary.'

'There is if you don't need to work. Your allowance from our father makes all this unnecessary.'

'I've simply had enough of lounging about poolsides. I need to do something, find myself a career.' Her face was earnest. 'I'm not the type to spend the rest of my life doing nothing. I've had that for two years now, it's time I did something useful.'

'You could always take Damien up on his offer.'

'*What?*' she asked sharply.

'Have that screen test,' he explained. 'I think you could be a success at it too.'

Kate sighed her relief. She had wondered what offer he meant for a moment, almost giving herself away. 'I've already told him I'm not interested in a screen test.' Or anything else he had to offer!

'You could change your mind.'

'But I haven't, I'm still not interested.' She broke off as she heard the doorbell ring. 'That will be Alan. Be nice to him, won't you?'

'Aren't I always nice to your friends?' He looked innocent.

Kate could remember a few occasions when he hadn't been, but she didn't remind him of them. 'I like Alan, I don't want you scaring him off.'

'As long as he isn't another Damien I won't interfere,' he promised.

'He's nothing like *him*,' she declared fiercely. 'Now behave!'

She rushed to open the door as the bell sounded again. 'Alan!' she smiled happily, reaching up to kiss him fleetingly on the lips, opening the door further for him to come inside.

Alan Reed was twenty-eight, a man who had worked himself up to being in charge of a large computer section in a flourishing firm. He carried himself with an authority Kate liked, remaining calm in any situation. He was tall and powerful, his body muscled, his light brown hair brushed casually back from his face and drawing attention to his deep blue eyes. He was good-looking without being conceited about it, always attentive, always courteous.

He turned now to pull her into his arms, demanding and receiving a lengthier kiss than he had received at the door. 'Mm,' he sighed against her lips. 'I've missed you.'

They hadn't seen each other for two days and she had missed him too, missed his companionship more than anything. 'James' car has broken down and I told him we'd give him a lift home. He's in the lounge.'

Alan took a step back. 'Oops, I didn't realise you had company.'

'It's only James,' she dismissed. 'I think we should leave now if you're ready. I should think he would like to shower and change before the rest of his guests arrive.'

'Yes, sure.'

'Come in and meet him,' Kate invited. 'I'll just get my fur jacket.'

She introduced the two men before disappearing into her bedroom. She couldn't help but feel relieved when she found them deep in conversation when she came back into the room. There could be no doubt that James approved of Alan, which was just as well, as she wasn't going to give him up. Alan was exactly what she needed to help her forget Damien, and she felt sure she would need his support this evening when she had to face Damien again.

She and Alan had been dating for about a month now, and while his kisses might not fire her as Damien's had she knew she was safe with him. He would never ask for more out of their friendship than she was prepared to give. She felt secure with him, happy and relaxed, something she had never felt with Damien.

She sat in the back of the car on the drive to the house, listening with interest to the conversation between the two men.

It was still only nine o'clock when they arrived, but already the house was full of people, the overflow gathered around the pool area. It was among one of these groups that they found Sheri.

'Darling!' she reached up to kiss her husband, moving away from her guests to be with him. 'I was beginning to get worried. I know you said you were coming with Kate, but I couldn't help wondering what had happened to you.'

He grimaced. 'Damien again! He's working the pants off everyone. He was still at it when I left.'

She smiled. 'He probably still is, he hasn't arrived here yet.'

'Maybe he won't bother. He hasn't been very sociable lately.'

That was probably the reason Kate hadn't met him at any of the other parties she had attended. She hadn't deliberately set out not to see him again, he just hadn't been around. Not that she for one moment thought he was carrying out his threat to avoid her. He probably had a new conquest and wanted to keep her to himself, and that was the reason for his unsociable behaviour. Whatever his reasons she hoped he didn't turn up tonight.

Sheri hugged James' arm to her side. 'Would you like me to get you something to eat?'

'I had something at the studio, thanks. But you can come along to the bedroom and help me change if you like.'

The glow in his grey eyes was wickedly inviting.

She giggled. 'Our guests, James!'

He looked around at the chattering, laughing people. 'They won't even notice we've gone.'

'Oh, James . . .'

'Come on.' He took a firm hold of her arm. 'No more arguments.'

Kate chuckled as the two disappeared into the house, smiling at Alan as he managed to get a couple of drinks for them from a passing waiter. 'You'll have to excuse them, they haven't been married very long.'

'They make a nice couple.' He looked curiously at the other guests. 'I would say James has quite an impressive guest list. So far I think we're the only two here whom I haven't either seen on the television or at the cinema. How come you got mixed up with this crowd?'

'Don't you like them?' She looked amused.

'I haven't spoken to any of them yet.'

She put her hand companionably through the crook of his arm. 'I'll take you round and introduce you to some of them.'

They were soon caught up in the laughing crowd, the place simply overflowing with people. They finally ended up in the largest room of the house where about fifty of the guests were attempting to dance. Kate and Alan finally gave up trying, simply swaying together to the music.

Alan grinned down at her. 'Like I said, how did you get mixed up with a mad crowd of people like this?'

'James is an old family friend,' she evaded. 'They're not so bad once you get to know them. They just work and play very hard.'

'Oh, I'm not complaining,' his smile was teasing. 'I'm enjoying the dancing immensely.'

She laughed up at him. 'Impossible, isn't it? Shall we——'

'Excuse me,' cut in a familiarly icy voice. 'Can I borrow

the lady for a dance or two?' drawled Damien Savage.

Kate's brown eyes flew open in alarm, the gold flecks more pronounced in her distress. 'I don't——'

Damien ignored her, pinpointing the other man with his inflexible green eyes. 'Do you have any objections?'

Alan looked taken aback by this arrogant man's persistence. 'I don't have any. But——'

'Good.' Damien effectively cut in front of him, pulling Kate roughly into his arms.

To be suddenly this close to him after not seeing him for so long made her tremble in his arms. He looked so attractive, dressed in white trousers and shirt, a royal blue velvet jacket fitting tautly across his shoulders. The shirt was opened casually at the throat, allowing her to see the beginning of the dark hairs that she knew ran across his chest and down past his navel. The thought of it made her tremble more than ever.

'Cold?' he murmured against her temple.

He knew very well she wasn't! 'A little,' she lied.

His answer was to pull her even closer, the firm outline of his thighs digging into her soft flesh. 'Better?' he asked softly.

She couldn't answer him, her emotions were running so high. He had no right to do this to her, no right to play on her senses like this. She cleared her throat before speaking. 'Actually, I was just going to sit down when you interrupted us.'

Damien looked down at her, his expression grim. 'Who was the man?'

'His name is Alan.' She avoided his eyes.

'You don't waste much time, do you? How does James feel about him?'

'James likes him.' She could feel the heat of his body through her clothing and it only unnerved her more. Her hands rested lightly on his shoulders, his own arms like steel bands about her slim body.

'Then he has more forbearance than I do,' he muttered. 'I can't bear to see any other man touch you.'

Kate tried to move away from him, but it wasn't very easy in this crush of people. 'Please don't start talking like that again. I don't feel the same way about it.'

'And this Alan,' he demanded, 'is he the marrying kind?'

'I believe so.'

'I know so,' he said roughly. 'You aren't marrying him, Kate. You aren't marrying anyone!'

This time she did pull out of his arms. 'I'll marry who I damn well please!'

The look in his eyes was frankly seductive, his mouth only inches away from her own. She looked around for Alan, but he seemed to have disappeared. Kate felt herself weakening towards Damien without the shield of Alan between them.

Damien slowly moved her into the curve of his arm, steering her out towards the pool. But they didn't stop there, Damien taking her out further to the garden and beyond. Finally he stopped, the noise of the party only a faint murmur in the distance.

Kate looked up at him with troubled brown eyes. 'Damien . . .'

'Oh, Kate!' He slowly bent his head to caress her throat with firm sensuous lips. 'I've missed you,' he admitted huskily.

Her protests died in her throat at the gentleness of his tone. Savagery might have evoked a much different response, but this gentleness she just couldn't fight. 'Did you really?' she asked softly, searching his arrogant features as if starved of the sight of him. And she was, she was just hungry for him. His harsh, sometimes cruel face was so dear to her, and for the moment she had forgotten Alan, had forgotten everyone but Damien.

'Can't you tell?' he asked ruefully. 'I'm sure James could

tell you I've been hell to work for the last few weeks.'

She gave a soft smile. 'He did.'

A certain grimness appeared about his mouth. 'When did you see James?'

She shrugged. 'This *is* his party.'

'I know that,' he said impatiently. 'But a party isn't exactly the sort of place you would hold that sort of conversation. Do you see a lot of him?'

'Quite a bit, yes.'

Damien's hold on her arms tightened. 'It has to stop, Kate. All these other men have to stop. I can't stand the sight of you with anyone else.'

She was beginning to feel mesmerised by the seduction evident in his eyes. 'Now look, Damien, I—I haven't seen you for over two months. You can't calmly walk back into my life and tell me to stop seeing people I happen to like very much.'

'I don't want you to see anyone but me,' he groaned. 'You're much too beautiful for my peace of mind. You ought to be locked up out of sight of other men. You've put me through hell the last few weeks. I can't eat, I can't sleep. Only work seems to dull the pain. I work until I'm so damned exhausted I collapse into a dreamless coma for a couple of hours.'

'Oh, Damien!' she was moved by the agony in his voice.

'Yes—oh, Damien,' he echoed derisively. 'You're so far into my system I can't think straight. And as for other women—forget it! I can't feel anything for them.'

'Oh, Damien,' she choked.

His mouth tightened and he pulled her roughly against him. 'Will you stop saying that! Just the sound of you saying my name is enough to turn me on.' His hands moved caressingly up her body, moulding her against the lean length of him. 'I'd love to hear you cry out my name as I made love to you.'

His words evoked pictures of the two of them together, rekindled thoughts she had striven to dampen over the past ten weeks.

'Won't you let me have you, Kate?' he pleaded against the softness of her throat, his lips seeming to burn where they touched.

'You know I can't,' she held on to the last of her sanity. 'I've already explained my reasons to you.'

'Damn your reasons!' He wrenched up her chin, his mouth savagely forcing her lips apart. When she groaned her pain relented slightly, his lips gently probing but his arms just as immovable.

Why must it always end like this, their being in each other's arms, their bodies crying out for each other? For Damien it was just basic lust, for her it was love. Both four-letter words and both so different in meaning. But such an important difference!

He was in complete control of her, moving her so that the grass was beneath her, Damien at her side. He turned her towards him, devouring her with that mouth that could look so cruel at times.

It seemed so long since she had been in his arms and it seemed so very right that they should be like this. Her hands were up about his neck, her fingers caressing his nape. His hair felt so thick and vital, so strong, like the rest of him.

She felt dizzy with desire, her body soft and pliant in his hands, her breasts pulsating with life beneath his probing fingers. Her clothing had been no barrier to his questing hands, the buttons down the front of her blouse easily undone and her breasts released to his searching lips.

She came up for air. 'Damien, please! You said you'd finished with me, that you didn't want any more to do with me.'

'I was wrong.' His lips strayed across her cheek, kissing each closed eyelid in turn. 'I can't stay away from you, I don't *want* to stay away. We both know what I want.'

'But I told you——'

'I know,' he silenced her with the pressure of his mouth on hers. 'But I've been thinking this thing out between us. I rushed you. You need time to get to know me.'

'No. I——' she shook her head. 'I don't need time.' She began to button her blouse with shaking fingers. 'Why can't you—why can't you stay away from me?' She felt so ashamed of what she had just let happen between them when she knew that was all he wanted from her. 'Why won't you accept no for an answer?'

'Because your body isn't saying no. You're a complete contradiction. Your eyes and mouth say no, but your body tells a different story.'

'That's because you're using all your experience on me. And you have plenty of that, don't you?' She stood up, brushing the grass from her skirt.

'Don't resort to insults, Kate. They aren't helping the situation.'

'Is it insulting to tell the truth?' She smoothed back her hair. God, she must look a mess!

There was no other way round this problem, she would have to stay away from Damien. Both of them had decided at different times that they weren't going to see each other again, that they wanted different things out of life, but neither of them seemed to have any control over the situation when they met. They just seemed to gravitate together and the only way to stop it was to stay away from each other.

Damien sighed, standing beside her now. There was still a glazed look in his eyes and his hands shook as he smoothed back his hair, the hair she had lovingly ruffled only seconds earlier.

'Don't kid yourself this is going to stop,' he warned her gruffly. 'It'll get worse before it gets better,' he assured her. 'Don't you think I haven't tried to get rid of this insatiable desire for you? Believe me, I've tried. I've taken out a dozen or more women in the last few weeks, they don't do a thing for me—except remind me of what I really want.'

Kate began walking back to the house. 'Then make love to one of them. But leave me alone!'

Damien swung her round to face him, his face ravaged, his eyes tortured. 'I'm trying to tell you—I can't take them! Nothing happens. Can you believe that?' He shook his head.

'With your reputation—no,' she said firmly.

'It's never happened to me before. I don't understand it myself.'

She resumed making her way to the house, the music and chatter becoming louder all the time. Whatever must Alan be thinking of her? She would find him and then they could leave. It must be getting quite late anyway.

'I don't want to understand it,' she dismissed. 'Now, if you'll excuse me, I have to find the man I came here with.'

Damien brought her up short with a grip on her arm. 'You mean you can just walk away from me, after what just happened?'

'Nothing happened,' she avoided his eyes.

He flung her away from him. 'Nothing happened!' he repeated violently. 'I nearly made love to you just now and you say nothing happened! What a cold little bitch you are!'

Cold! That was the last thing she was. She had felt aflame since the first time she had met him, and each time it grew worse. 'If you like to think so,' she agreed distantly.

'Kate,' he groaned her name. 'You can't go!'

Well, she certainly couldn't stay! He was tearing her apart. She wanted to get back to Alan, where she felt safe. She gave Damien one last look before walking off to find Alan.

She hurried into what had once been her bedroom, blushing anew at the sight that met her in the mirror. Her hair was in complete disorder and she had a wild untamed look about her eyes. Her cheeks were flaming and her mouth had a kissed, bruised look. She looked exactly what she was, a girl who had been kissed until she was almost senseless.

Oh, Damien ... She sat down on the bed, her shoulders slumped, her look one of utter defeat. If Damien were to come in here now she would surrender herself to him without a word—anything to stop this gnawing ache inside of her.

Her head shot up as the door opened softly, the gladness leaving her face as she saw who it was. 'Matt Strange!' she breathed his name with disbelief, feeling as if she had played this scene once before.

He walked arrogantly into the room, completely sure of himself. 'The one and only,' he slurred the words. The drink in his hand was evidence of his inebriated state. And he was one man who didn't need alcohol to give him confidence, he had enough of that already.

Kate just wasn't in the mood for him. To be perfectly truthful she had really become fed up with him in the last few weeks. He seemed to turn up at every party she went to, always making his interest in her plain. Well, she didn't like him and she just couldn't hide these feelings.

She repressed a shiver of revulsion towards him, not liking the look in his eyes at all. 'Shall we rejoin the party?' she asked him as politely as she was able.

'Not so fast.' His hand shot out and he pinned her against the wall with his body. 'Been out for a little tussle on the grass with Damien?' he taunted, breathing whisky fumes all over her.

It was so near the truth and so crudely put that the hot colour quickly flooded her cheeks. 'Don't be so disgusting!' she snapped, finding it impossible to escape from the circle of his arms.

He gave a lopsided grin. 'You like calling me disgusting, don't you? That's the second time you've done it.'

'Possibly because you are,' Kate said coolly.

'But I'm right, aren't I?' he taunted. 'I've been watching you all evening. That poor sap you came here with has no idea what you're like, has he? He's been looking for you for the past hour. But don't worry, I didn't tell him about you and Damien.'

'Well, thank you,' she said sarcastically. 'That was so kind of you.'

Her sarcasm was lost on him in his drunken state. 'If he doesn't have the intelligence to realise you've been missing for the last hour then he doesn't deserve to know,' he slurred. 'But I know, Kate. And I still want to know when it's going to be my turn.'

Her head snapped back angrily. 'I don't like you, Mr Strange. I never have. Now will you kindly take your hands off me or must I scream as I did the last time you tried something like this?'

'I think that would be rather silly, don't you?' He bent to kiss her throat with wet lips. 'I may not be Damien Savage, but I'm sure I could please you just as much as he does.'

'I doubt it,' she answered dryly, squirming away from those horrible lips, but her movements only seemed to excite him more.

'So do I,' drawled an icy voice.

Matt Strange turned to face Damien, the drink giving him more courage than he might otherwise have felt against such a ruthless, arrogant man. 'Get out of here, Damien,' he ordered. 'You aren't wanted.'

'I might agree with you if Kate looked a little more as if she was enjoying having you touch her. But she doesn't,' Damien added harshly. 'And unless you want me to put you on the floor again I would advise *you* to get out.'

'You mean you haven't finished with her yet?' Matt asked insultingly. 'She's lasted a long time. She must be good.'

It was so far from the truth that Kate almost laughed, a hysterical laugh, but nevertheless a laugh. And she knew Damien was thinking along the same lines because of the mocking lift to his mouth.

'Go and sober up, Matt,' he advised. 'You have to be on the set at seven o'clock tomorrow morning. And I won't accept any excuses for your being late.'

'One of these days, Damien . . .' Matt threatened.

'Yeah, yeah, I've heard it all before. You can forget the insulting names too, save them for some other time.'

'God, you're an arrogant bast——'

Damien's jaw tightened. 'I said I'd pass on the name-calling,' he repeated softly. 'You have precisely five seconds to get out of here.'

Matt went, probably remembering the last time he had crossed this man. And also remembering the painful swollen nose he had sported for days, the bruising had taken weeks to fade properly.

Kate gave a relieved smile. 'It seems I have to thank you once again. And I do—most sincerely. He——'

Damien gave her a look of utter disgust. 'Don't try explaining him away a second time. Matt was going to give you exactly what you've been asking for for weeks. I'd oblige you myself, but I've suddenly gone off the idea. Maybe now that I can see the full extent of what you are, the way you deliberately encourage a man and then watch as he squirms, maybe now I can forget you. I was right about you, you have a complex about men. You like to hurt us.'

She gasped. 'That isn't true!'

He ran a weary hand across his furrowed brow. 'Emasculated for a little tease!' He shook his head. 'One of these days you're going to push one of us too far and find yourself raped.'

He slammed the door behind him as he left and Kate burst into tears. What a traumatic time it had been for her since Damien came into her life. But it didn't have to be! All she had to do was say yes to him and everything would change. At least, that was all she had had to do; Damién denied even wanting her now.

And the fact that he was dancing so close to a tall black-haired girl when she came into the room five minutes later seemed to confirm what he had said. He was nibbling the girl's earlobe and she was giggling happily, her arms about his waist under his velvet jacket.

Kate's face twisted with pain as she turned away, search-ing much more avidly for Alan now. She couldn't stay here and watch Damien with another woman, not when she wanted so desperately herself to be the one in his arms.

'Here you are.' Alan hugged her to him. 'I've been look-ing for you everywhere. Where have you been?'

She deliberately didn't look up into his honest uncompli-cated face, hating herself for having to lie to him. But she could hardly tell him the truth! 'I've been looking for you too. We must have kept missing each other.'

'I suppose so,' he agreed slowly.

'I'd like to leave, if you don't mind?'

'No, I don't mind at all. I'd like to be alone with you for a while.' The gleam in his eyes told her the reason why.

Kate just wanted to get away from the sight of that girl snuggled in Damien's arms as he whispered in her ear. She just couldn't bear to look at them another moment longer.

She laughed up at Alan. 'Okay, let's find James and make our excuses.'

They were soon on their way back to her flat and the tension began to leave her rigidly held body. She would have to stop tormenting herself with thoughts of Damien. It would have to stop!

'That man,' Alan broke into her thoughts. 'The one who asked you to dance. Who was he? He looked familiar, but I can't place him.'

'Damien Savage,' she supplied shortly.

Alan whistled through his teeth. 'And how do you know him?'

'He's a friend of James',' she replied abruptly, staring straight ahead.

'He's a handsome specimen.' He looked at her probingly.

'If you like men who are bossy and overbearing.'

'And don't you—like him, I mean?'

'Why should I?' she asked tartly.

'I asked first,' he said softly.

Kate gave a short mirthless laugh. 'Why all the questions, Alan? Surely you aren't jealous, are you?'

'Of Damien Savage?' He shrugged nonchalantly. 'Of course I am! Someone like him comes up and walks off with my girl, how do you expect me to feel?'

'Surely you could tell I didn't want to dance with him?'

'That was what I thought. But then you disappeared with him—at least, I suppose it was with him. You both disappeared at the same time.'

'Damien can be very—dominant. But I got away from him as soon as I possibly could. Are you coming in for coffee?' she asked as they reached her flat.

He nodded his agreement, locking the car before following her into the lift. The coffee made, they sat down to chat. Alan stayed for an hour or so, lingering over their parting.

'See you tomorrow?' he murmured against her lips.

'Mm, come round for lunch. Josie's going down to Kent tomorrow to meet Paul's parents, so we'll have the flat to ourselves.'

He quirked an eyebrow. 'That sounds nice.'

Kate laughed huskily at his expression. 'I hope I can trust you to behave.'

'Don't I always?' He kissed her gently.

'Yes.'

He lifted her chin, laughing a little. 'Hey, don't sound so disappointed!'

She wasn't disappointed, she just wished that for once, he would try to sweep her off her feet. That way he might erase Damien from her mind and body.

She pretended to be asleep when Josie got home, her face turned firmly against the wall, not in the mood for girlish chatter this evening. But she lay awake long after Josie had gone to her own room, her eyes wide as she admitted to herself that Alan's kisses had in no way helped to blot out the feel of Damien's burning lips upon her own. She doubted that any man's kisses could do that.

CHAPTER EIGHT

'I INSIST that you stay to dinner,' Sheri told her. 'James should be home soon and I know he'd love to see you. You haven't been over much lately.'

Kate hadn't been over because she didn't want to run the risk of accidentally running into Damien here. 'Well, I have started my secretarial course now and I go out with Alan quite a lot in the evenings.' Although not so much of late.

'How's the secretarial course going?'

'All right, but there's an awful lot to learn, much more than I realised.'

'And how are things with Alan?'

Kate wished she knew. They went out together two, maybe three times a week, she enjoyed being with him, and she responded reasonably well to his kisses. But that was where the trouble between them lay. She knew Alan was starting to wonder at her lack of ardour, that the light lovemaking between them did not fire her as the merest touch from Damien could do.

She was beginning to wonder if she was being fair to Alan, if she wasn't using him as a shield against her real feelings. She did enjoy being with him, yes, but she enjoyed being with Damien more.

Damien! Why did he have to keep intruding into her life? That he was back on his usual social whirl she knew, pictures of him dining out or at the theatre with one girl or another often appearing in the daily newspapers. He was a celebrity and his activities were definitely news, red-hot news some of it.

Actually she hadn't seen Alan for the last three days, but

they were meeting later this evening. She would have to make sure she was back in town for that. 'Things are fine between Alan and me,' she finally answered.

'And Damien?' Sheri probed.

'What about him?' she asked sharply.

Sheri shrugged. 'I had the feeling a couple of months back that you were rather keen on him.'

Kate attempted a light laugh. 'He's every girl's dream. I was bound to be bowled over by his interest in me. I used to dream about meeting him when I was a child—you know the fantasies we have at twelve and thirteen.'

'And he didn't live up to them?'

He more than lived up to them! He was larger than life, very sexy, and totally immoral. He was the sort of man who didn't think marriage was necessary and indulged in numerous affairs.

'You know he did,' she admitted softly. 'But you must know what he's like.'

'I know what he's like now. James hardly ever gets home before eight o'clock in the evening, and he's always tired out when he gets in. Damien's just gone overboard for work.'

'So James said the other week. I suppose that's how Damien got to the top in his profession.'

Sheri frowned. 'He's playing hard too. He never goes out with the same woman twice.'

Kate gave a bitter laugh. 'I don't suppose he needs to if he gets what he wants the first time around.'

'Oh dear, he has made a bad impression with you! I told you from the first that he's a very blunt person.'

He was blunt to the point of being rude, never mixing his words when talking to her, making his impression of her very clear. 'How's the film going?' Kate changed the subject.

Sheri shrugged. 'James says very well. But the tension between Matt and Damien is reaching exploding point.'

Damien again! She grimaced. 'Couldn't we leave him out of the conversation?'

Sheri giggled. 'It's impossible with James. For the first ten minutes when he gets home he does nothing but complain about him. You wait and see—I don't think tonight will be any different. He was going to insist on getting home by seven tonight, so he'll probaby have a blazing row with Damien so that he can get away.'

'Is he really that bad?'

'Impossible,' Sheri confirmed.

The two of them were seated in the lounge, Kate having arrived after lunch to spend the afternoon with Sheri. Her sister-in-law was occasionally a little lonely during the day now that she had given up her modelling career and so Kate had decided to help occupy one afternoon for her.

James had asked Sheri to give up her career so that they might be together when he wasn't working. Sheri had enough sense to realise that two people working extensively here and abroad, often at different times, found it difficult to make a success of a marriage. She acknowledged the fact that while her career had been enjoyable it wasn't to be her whole life. They hoped to have a family soon, so it was James' career that was important for the moment.

'I can't be too late home,' Kate said. 'Alan's coming over about eight-thirty.'

'James promised he would get home early, and I'm sure he will because I told him I was going to try and persuade you to stay for dinner. He misses you, you know.'

'I miss him too,' Kate admitted.

'We would like you to move back here with us.'

Kate was touched by the sincerity of her words, but she shook her head firmly. 'I couldn't let James take over my life again. You know what he used to be like.'

'Mm, I——' Sheri broke off. 'I think that's him now. Go and meet him,' she encouraged.

'Wouldn't you like to go?'

'I'll see him in a minute. I know he's been looking for-ward to seeing you. You found each other so late in life that I'm afraid he'll always be this protective of you. He loves you, Kate. Try to understand him.'

Kate swallowed an emotional lump in her throat, stand-ing up to go and meet her brother. 'I wonder if he realises how well you know him.'

'I think so,' Sheri said softly.

'Well, I hope he realises how lucky he is.'

She laughed. 'Go and meet him.'

Kate hurried to the door, hearing the faint murmur of voices in the entrance-hall. 'Now then, James,' she laughed, 'Sheri and I have decided that we don't want any talk about your demonic director this evening,' she laughed lightly. 'We all know what a bully and a tyrant he——'

She broke off in dismay, a dark colour staining her cheeks as she saw who was with her brother. Damien Savage! And look at the way she had just spoken about him!

James gave a throaty chuckle at her confusion. 'As you can see, I brought Damien with me.'

'The demonic director,' Damien drawled mockingly.

The colour stayed in her cheeks. 'I didn't realise you were with James.'

'Would it have made any difference if you had?'

She held her head high. 'Probably not.'

He gave a half smile. 'I didn't think so.'

Sheri had left the lounge to see what was going on, moving over to kiss her husband before greeting her guest. It gave Kate the chance to study Damien without being observed.

He was still as attractive as ever, but he looked different. The lines of cynicism about his mouth and nose had deep-ened and there were lines of strain about his eyes. His hair was still as thick and vital, but she could see a few strands of grey among its blackness. And he looked leaner too, his muscles more pronounced. As Sheri had already said, he looked as if he was working and playing too hard, mainly playing, she would hazard.

'It's lovely to see you again, Damien,' Sheri said with a smile.

'Even if I am the demonic director?' he taunted.

She laughed. 'Don't be cruel and remind Kate of her mistake,' she rebuked him.

'She seems to make a lot of them where I'm concerned,' he drawled.

Kate blushed, her embarrassment momentarily covered by James' bear-like hug and the firm kiss he planted on her cheek. He stood back, surveying her censoriously. 'You don't look well,' he stated abruptly.

She put up a hand to her pale cheeks, the surprise of seeing Damien beginning to fade. 'I'm fine, James.'

'No, you're not. Are you working too hard?'

She could sense Damien watching the two of them and it took a strong effort of will not to meet that challenging look. 'I'm not working at all, I'm only learning at the moment.'

'Well, it doesn't agree with you. With your allowance you have no need to work. By the time you've finished this course you'll probably decide to get married, then you won't need it.'

'I have no intention of getting married.'

'That's what I said,' he scoffed, 'and look what happened to me!'

'What course are you taking?' Damien interrupted harshly.

'A secretarial course,' she supplied unwillingly.

The mockery increased in his green eyes. 'I don't think you're the secretary type.' The look in his eyes told her he pictured her in quite another role.

'I'd better go and change for dinner,' James said ruefully.

'That reminds me,' Damien voiced softly, 'I still have a pair of your trousers.'

James frowned. 'A pair of my—— How on earth did you get a pair of my trousers?'

Damien quirked an eyebrow. 'I should ask Kate that.'

So it was to be that way, was it! Well, she was far from admitting defeat. She threw back her head defiantly. 'I let Damien borrow a pair of your trousers when he got his own wet at your apartment.'

Sheri looked puzzled. 'How did he do that? Or is that an embarrassing question?'

Damien gave a soft laugh. 'I believe it is.'

'I see.' James bit his lip, obviously remembering the occasion alluded to. 'I'll go and change.'

'I'll come with you,' his wife said hurriedly, feeling an unwanted third.

'Does James always try and ignore your little discrepancies?' Damien rasped once they were alone.

'I've already explained to him about that night and morning.'

'And he believed you?'

'He had no reason not to,' she said softly.

'I would have thought there were two very good reasons —I'm a man and you're a woman.'

'I've told you before, that doesn't necessarily mean what smutty little minds take it to mean. Shall we go into the lounge and wait for the others?'

He followed her, sitting down as she did the same. 'I'll never understand this set-up.'

'I wouldn't even try,' she derided.

'Are you still seeing—what's his name, Alan, was it?'

'Yes, it was, and yes, I am.'

'And you haven't missed me at all?' he asked softly, watching her intently.

'Was I supposed to?' Kate couldn't help her surprise.

Each time they parted Damien made his intention of never seeing her again perfectly clear.

'Maybe,' he said nonchalantly. 'Did you?'

'No,' she lied.

Sheri came back into the room at that moment. 'Jennings says dinner is ready. Shall we all go through to the dining-room?'

Kate ate hardly anything of the beautifully prepared meal, all too much aware of Damien sitting just across the table from her. His personality reached out and touched her, making it impossible for her to ignore him, no matter how much she tried.

Sheri poured out their coffee as they were seated in the lounge. 'Did you borrow James' trousers the weekend you took Kate away?' she asked conversationally, obviously curious about them, having received no information from her husband. Besides, the intent looks Damien was giving Kate were not going unnoticed by James—and he was getting angrier by the minute.

'Yes,' Damien answered shortly, still looking at Kate.

'Do you have to make it sound like that?' James demanded of his wife. 'It was all perfectly innocent.'

Sheri wasn't sure this could be true, not by the look of embarrassment on Kate's face and the look of derision in Damien's eyes. 'I only mentioned it because that weekend has happy memories for me. That was the weekend we got engaged.'

She saw her husband's face darken and the sharp look Damien gave him and she wondered what she had said wrong this time. Kate merely looked resigned, and Sheri's puzzlement grew.

Damien looked at her now. 'You got engaged that weekend?'

Kate felt sorry for her sister-in-law, she could have no idea what she had just done. Herself, she felt relieved the truth was at last coming out, but James just looked angry. She wasn't sure how Damien had reacted to this information; after his first initial surprise his expression had become deadpan.

'Yes,' Sheri smiled happily.

'I somehow thought it was much later than that,' Damien persisted.

'No, that was the weekend James popped the question.' She gave her husband a loving smile which he reluctantly returned, realising that he couldn't stop the truth coming out now. 'You probably got that impression because I had to return to the States to fulfil a contract and so the engagement wasn't actually announced until later. I left the day after we got engaged and was away a few weeks.'

Poor Sheri, she had quite innocently made her husband out to be a liar. Not that Kate minded, it just proved to Damien that she had been telling the truth when she had told him she had never had any intention of marrying James. Not that it would make the slightest difference to Damien's opinion of her, but at least in that he would know she hadn't been lying.

She looked at her wrist-watch; it was getting quite late and she would have to get back to town for her date with Alan. She stood up, making her excuses. 'I've enjoyed my dinner,' she added politely.

James stood up too. 'You won't leave it so long next time? A week is much too long for you to stay away.'

'I'll be over again in the next few days,' she promised.

'I'll drive you back to town,' Damien offered softly.

She gave him a cool look, steadily meeting his probing green eyes. 'That won't be necessary. I have my own car.' It was a green Spitfire, an eighteenth birthday present from James.

His mouth tightened. 'Then I'll meet you back in town. I want to talk to you.'

'That isn't possible either, I'm afraid,' she refused.

Damien's look was challenging. 'Why not?'

'I'm meeting someone. That's why I have to leave so early.'

'Alan?' For the moment the two of them had forgotten they were not alone, the old antagonism and attraction coming to the fore.

Kate blushed. 'That's right.'

'Have you met him?' James broke up the intimacy of their conversation. 'Nice chap, isn't he?'

The look he received from the other man was glacial. 'I've hardly spoken to him.' But that Damien disliked the man was obvious.

'Oh. I just assumed——'

'Well, don't,' Damien told him shortly. 'I have to be going now too. Thank you for the dinner, Sheri. I hope you'll all excuse me.'

His departure was so abrupt that for a few minutes none of them spoke, staring in amazement at the firmly closed door.

'Well!' James finally burst out. 'The nerve of the man!'

'Now come on, James,' Sheri chided. 'It wasn't wholly his fault. You set out to antagonise him from the start, pushing Alan down his throat when even a blind man could see he fancies Kate like mad.'

'That's *why* I pushed Alan down his throat. I don't like him chasing my sister.'

'You made that pretty obvious,' she returned dryly. 'And I didn't help the situation. What did I say to upset him, Kate?' She looked at her pleadingly. 'He suddenly went all narrow-eyed and watchful.'

Kate shook her head. 'I think you should ask your devious husband that—he's the one with all the answers. Now I really do have to get back to town or Alan will think I've stood him up. I'm probably going to be late as it is.'

That Sheri wouldn't rest until she had extracted everything from James Kate had no doubt, but she didn't have the time to stay around and watch the fun. One thing she was sure of, Sheri would have little patience with James' interference.

Alan was sitting in his car outside her apartment when she arrived home. She invited him in, pouring him out a whisky before sitting down next to him on the sofa.

'I'm sorry I'm late, darling.' She leant against his chest, his arm about her shoulders. 'I spent the afternoon with Sheri.'

'Have a nice time?'

'Yes, thank you. It was just the usual girlish chatter, but I did enjoy myself.' Until it came to dinner!

'Good. I'm glad.'

Kate looked at him sharply. There was something wrong. Alan wasn't his usual cheerful self. And now she came to think about it his hello kiss had been much more restrained than normal.

'Is there anything wrong?' she asked him worriedly.

He looked down at her vaguely. 'Wrong? Why should there be anything wrong?'

She sat up on the sofa, her legs tucked beneath her. 'You're different, I can tell that. What's happened?'

Alan removed his arm from about her with a sigh. 'Am I that transparent?'

'Just tell me what's wrong.'

He put up a hand to gently caress her cheek, a look of tenderness for her in his face. 'Why couldn't you have loved me?' he mused softly. 'One little show of love on your part and I would have been your slave for life.'

'What do you mean, Alan?' she asked.

'I mean that if you were going to fall in love with me there would have been some sign of it by now,' he sighed again. 'But there hasn't been. I'm just wasting my time with you.'

She gently kissed his hand where he touched her. 'I like you tremendously, Alan, you know that.'

He took her roughly by the shoulders, shaking her slightly. 'It isn't enough, Kate. Liking me isn't enough!'

'But what can I do about it? What do you *want* me to do about it?'

'There's nothing you can do. It's that other man, of course. You're in love with him,' he scowled.

Kate moved out of his grasp to stand up, her hands kneading together nervously. 'What other man?' she evaded.

'Damien Savage,' he said harshly.

She gave a light choking laugh. 'You're being ridiculous! I don't love——'

'Yes, you do! I saw your reaction to him at that party, saw the way he looked at you too. How long did you go out with him?'

'I've only ever been out with him the once.' But she had seen him so many other times, and each time her love for him deepened.

It seemed her decision that she wasn't being fair to Alan was being taken out of her hands. From the way he was talking she had the feeling he was going to finish with her, not the other way round. But perhaps it was as well it should happen this way.

'That once was enough for you to fall for him.'

'Maybe you're right,' she admitted gently.

'I know I am.'

She looked at him with anguished eyes. 'But that doesn't stop me liking you! And we—we've had fun together, haven't we?'

'Yes, but now that has to stop. I have to be honest with you and say it isn't only because of Savage that I don't think we should meet again.' He looked embarrassed, his blue eyes troubled. 'I—I've been meeting someone else.'

'I see.'

'She's someone I met at work,' he explained hurriedly. 'I've taken her out a couple of times during the last few weeks. Sue's more my type, Kate. I don't fit in with the theatrical crowd you mix with.'

'But that's the reason why I——'

'Why you first started going out with me,' he finished for her. 'I know that, I've always known it. And I suppose at first I was attracted to the glamour surrounding you. You're really something special, I hope you know that. I still liked you even when I got past the glamour, and as I said, given the right encouragement I could so easily have fallen in love with you.'

'But I didn't give the right encouragement?'

'I was quite hopeful until I met Damien Savage, but after that I knew I didn't stand a chance. I've just been kidding myself all these weeks.'

Kate cleared her throat; she was going to miss Alan in her life. 'And Sue, what's she like?'

The gentle smile he gave told her just how fond of the other girl he really was—and the fact that she felt no pain at this knowledge just confirmed how little her own affections had been involved.

'She's small, with glossy black hair and laughing brown eyes. She's just an ordinary girl, I suppose,' he shrugged.

She gave him a soft smile. 'I'm glad for you, Alan, really glad.'

'We aren't getting serious or anything like that,' he went on. 'It's much too early to know our feeling for each other yet. But I—I thought I should tell you the truth.'

'Thank you.' She reached up to kiss him lightly on the lips. 'It was very nice of you to come over and tell me.'

'Yes, well, I—I suppose I'd better be going.'

She burst into tears once he had left, more because she suddenly felt so lonely than because she had been upset about their parting. She was upset, but the outcome had always been inevitable. If she had been going to get over these feelings she had for Damien she would have done so by now, and it just wasn't right to use another man as a shield against these feelings.

It was still so early, only nine-thirty, what could she do to pass the time? It was much too early to go to bed and yet too late to go out again. In the end she decided to wash her hair, have a long leisurely bath, and give her nails a manicure. Not that there was much left of her nails, the typing she did at college had effectively broken most of them. But it was something to do, something to take her mind off being lonely.

Eleven o'clock saw her firmly tucked up in bed, tired of attempting to read and trying very hard to fall asleep instead. She wasn't doing a very good job of that either, and she struggled thankfully out of bed as she heard the insistent ringing of the doorbell. Josie had probably forgotten her key again. She was a lovely girl and a true friend, but she did have the most shocking memory.

Kate hurried out of her bedroom, eager to answer the door before Josie gave up, thinking that she herself wasn't home yet. She released the lock on the door and moved back quickly as it slammed back with a loud thud.

Swaying slightly in the doorway, his eyes grim and red-rimmed, stood Damien Savage. He had a wild look in his eyes and as he pushed past her Kate was distressed to realise he had been drinking—and heavily, by the look of him. He reeked of whisky, and she followed him nervously as he strolled uninvited into the lounge. He had made no move to close the door after his unwanted entrance, so Kate closed it with a slam before hurrying after him.

He swung round to look at her, his smart appearance of earlier much less immaculate now. His shirt was almost fully unbuttoned, his trousers very creased. He looked her up and down as she clutched the sheer nightdress to her otherwise naked body. She hadn't thought a wrap was necessary just to let Josie into the flat, but she wished she had thought better of it now. By the look in Damien's eyes she might as well not have bothered with the nightdress either.

'What are you doing here?' she demanded, attempting to feel outraged but finding that fear was her predominant feeling, fear of that look in his eyes.

'That's a damn stupid question to ask me,' he sneered. 'Where is he? Still in the bedroom?'

Her mouth fell open in surprise. 'What are you talking about?'

If it was possible he sneered even more. 'Your lover— this Alan you seem to find pleasure in tormenting me with.' His voice was decidedly slurred, even more evidence of his having been drinking.

'You're drunk,' she accused.

He threw back his head with a harsh laugh. 'Of course I'm drunk! What the hell else do you expect me to be?'

She took an involuntary step towards him, flinching as he pushed her away. 'Damien, what's wrong?'

'What's wrong?' he repeated scathingly. 'You left James' house this evening with the intention of jumping straight into bed with this Alan you seem to find so attractive—of course I've been drinking! I've been trying to forget exactly what you are and what you've been doing all evening.'

Kate shook her head, staring at him disbelievingly. 'You don't know what you're saying.'

'Like hell I don't!' He looked towards her bedroom, the glowing light in there evidence of her recent occupation. 'What's he doing, hiding in the bedroom?'

'There's no one here but us,' she denied.

'I can't believe he's left already.' He staggered over to the bedroom door and kicked it open with his foot. 'Well, well, well.' He walked into the room, looking about him inter- estedly. 'So you really were alone.'

'I told you I was.' Kate held the bedroom door open pointedly. 'Now if you wouldn't mind removing yourself?'

'Oh, but I do, I mind very much.' He sat down on the bed, patting the space beside him. 'Come over here.'

Her eyes widened. 'No!'

He lay back on the rumpled bedclothes. 'Mmm, quite comfortable.' His voice seemed to be becoming fainter and Kate's face mirrored her dismay. He just couldn't pass out here!

She rushed over to his side, trying unsuccessfully to pull him to his feet. 'You can't fall asleep here,' she said desperately. 'Please, Damien! Get up.'

His answer was to give her hand a sharp tug, unbalancing her so that she fell on top of him. With a swiftness she wouldn't have believed him capable of in his inebriated state he rolled over, pinning her beneath him.

'Damien!' she pleaded.

There was no mercy for her in those narrowed green eyes as he bent his head to kiss her throat. 'Damien what?' he muttered. 'Damien, leave me alone? Or Damien, love me?' He continued with his caressing lips down to the hollow between her breasts.

'Damien, I——' she groaned as he touched her breasts with his mouth, coaxing them to full pulsating life, her denials for his touch dying on her lips.

'Damien, love me,' he answered for her throatily. 'I intend to, angel. I intend to love you all the way to hell and back.'

'Hell?' she asked breathlessly.

'I'm going to give you some of the hell you've put me through since I met you. Oh, Kate,' he moaned against her lips. 'I've got to have you, whether it be willingly or a fight to the end.'

He took her lips with a savagery that told her he wasn't going to be gentle with her, that his taking of her was to be a punishment. A trip to hell he had described it, and she could well believe he meant it.

'No, Damien!' She began pushing at him. 'Not like this.'

'*Exactly* like this,' he told her between gritted teeth. 'You won't taunt and tease me again, that I can promise you.'

Her whimper of pain as he pinned her to the bed was unheard by him. He was intent only on taking her body, his lips painful and brutal. Finally, when she thought she could fight him no longer, she felt the life go out of him, his body suddenly heavy on hers.

'Damien?' she queried tentatively, not sure if this was another trick. She said his name again when he didn't answer her, but there was still no reply. There could be no doubt about it, he had passed out.

It took all her strength to push him off her, but finally she managed it. He must have had a lot to drink for it to have affected him like this! It was impossible to wake him, so in the end she gave up trying. He would have to stay here for the night. She could sleep on the sofa.

She made him more comfortable before leaving the room, slipping off his shoes before sliding his legs on to the bed. She wished she could take off his jacket, but he was much too heavy for her to move. Oh well, it served him right if he ached in the morning. She had no sympathy for him.

She was still shaking when she came out of the bedroom, turning out the light and closing the door behind her. Damien was going to have the devil of a headache in the morning. And so he ought to have!

Kate was sipping a cup of coffee when Josie came in, her nerves slowly steadying. She had no doubt that if Damien hadn't passed out he would have carried out his threat. There had been a steely inflexibility that would have ignored her protests.

Wordlessly she poured Josie a cup of coffee from the pot, still too shaken to engage in polite conversation.

'Thanks.' Josie sipped the brew. 'There's a fantastic car outside,' she exclaimed excitedly. 'Paul and I have just been looking at it. I wonder if it belongs to someone living in the building.'

'No,' Kate answered dully.

'Do you know who it belongs to?' Josie looked at her interestedly.

'Yes.'

'Who?'

'Him.' Kate nodded in the direction of her bedroom.

Josie's eyes widened. 'Who?' she squeaked.

'Damien Savage.' Kate picked up her coffee mug, washing and drying it before putting it away. 'And before you jump to the wrong conclusion I think I should just explain that I didn't invite him here. And he's in my bed because that's where he passed out.'

Josie frowned. 'But how did he get——' she broke off in embarrassment.

Kate sighed. 'Now that's something I *don't* intend going into. Just except that he's there and I intend sleeping on the sofa.'

'Are you sure? We could probably both get into my bed.'

'No, I'll stay out here. I'll have to keep an eye on our unwanted guest, he may start wandering in the night.'

Josie giggled. 'Well, if he does, steer him in my direction!'

'Josie!'

'Well,' Josie smiled sheepishly, 'I think he's gorgeous. Really fantastic looking.'

'Mm, maybe.' Kate got on the sofa, pulling the blankets over her that she had collected from the linen cupboard. She yawned tiredly. 'Put the light out, Josie, there's a love.'

Josie looked disappointed. 'Oh—okay. See you in the morning.'

As soon as Josie had left all tiredness left her too. She would certainly have a few things to say to Damien in the morning.

Morning seemed a long time coming round; she could find little rest in her sleepless tossing and turning on a sofa

that suddenly seemed to have developed numerous lumps
and bumps she had never noticed before.

By seven o'clock she had had enough, and moved quietly
about as she dressed, not wanting to wake Josie. She made
two mugs of coffee and carried them over to her bedroom.
She closed the door firmly behind her. What she had to
say to Damien was totally private.

She looked down at him as he still slept, the dark stubble
on his chin evidence of his night's sleep. Some time during
the night he had discarded his jacket and shirt, although
his trousers still remained. Kate allowed herself a few
minutes of just looking at him, at his strong tanned chest
and the dark good looks of him. For a few minutes she
looked down at him tenderly, and then the remembrance
of last night came back to her and she slammed his coffee
mug down right next to his ear.

Damien stirred druggingly, opening bleary green eyes
and sitting up gingerly as he tried to focus on her. That he
had a king-size headache was obvious, and he drank his
coffee thirstily before attempting to speak. 'Good morning,'
he said groggily.

'Good morning!' Kate dismissed scoffingly.

He pushed back his ruffled hair, rubbing his aching
temples. 'Okay, so there's nothing good about it. But do
you have to shout about it?'

'I wasn't shouting!'

He tried to open his eyes to their full extent and failed,
groaning as she callously pulled back the curtains, allowing
the early morning light to penetrate every corner of the
room. 'You bitch!' he swore at her.

'If you can't take your drink you shouldn't attempt to
try,' she told him curtly. 'Now would you mind getting out
of my bed and then out of my flat?'

'I'd mind a great deal.' He winced as he swung his legs to
the floor. 'What happened here last night?'

Kate looked at him sharply. 'You mean you don't remember?'

Damien gave her an impatient look. 'Would I be asking if I did?'

She gave a careless shrug. 'You burst into this flat last night hurling abuse and intending to make love to me, by force if necessary.'

He looked pointedly at the rumpled bed. 'Would it be asking too much to hope that I succeeded?'

'You didn't,' she told him shortly.

'Pity.' He raised dark eyebrows at her. 'Why didn't I?'

'Mainly because you passed out and secondly because I didn't want you to.'

'I see.' He looked at her thoughtfully. 'Did I ask you anything last night?'

'You asked me several things. Like, where my lover was, if he was still here. You asked me that quite a lot.'

He ran a tired hand over his aching eyes. 'God, my head hurts! And that wasn't the type of question I meant. Did I ask you anything—anything more personal?'

She gave a short derisive laugh. 'What could be more personal than that?'

He stood up with an effort. 'Will you pull those damned curtains! The light's killing me,' he snapped.

Sighing, she did so. 'You shouldn't have drunk so much.'

'I drank so much because you're driving me quietly insane. I can't take any more, Kate. I give in.'

Her eyes widened. 'What do you mean?'

'I mean exactly what I say. I give in. I'll marry you. That was what I meant to ask you last night, but I guess I wasn't in any fit state to do it. I'll marry you, Kate—any time you say.'

CHAPTER NINE

SHE stared at him aghast. Had Damien really said he would *marry* her? Yes, he had said that, exactly that. Not that he wanted to marry her, but that he would. It wasn't her idea of a proposal.

'You have to be joking,' she said scathingly.

Damien arched his neck, running a hand round the back of his head to his tired nape. God, how he ached everywhere. 'Did I sound as if I were joking?' he asked disgustedly, feeling as if he could drink a gallon of coffee and still feel lousy.

'Well, no. But you——'

'Then don't be so damned stupid!' he snapped impatiently. 'I'm hardly in the mood to indulge in that sort of humour at the moment.' He flexed his shoulders, his muscles rippling under his tanned skin. 'God, your bed's uncomfortable! How on earth do you sleep in it?'

'You seemed to consider it very comfortable last night, comfortable enough for two in fact. And you don't appear to have had any trouble sleeping in it. Uncomfortable though it may appear to you, I would have preferred to be sleeping in it rather than trying to sleep on the sofa.'

He focused on her with an effort. 'You could have shared the bed with me—the offer was there, and it wouldn't have been the first time,' he taunted.

'That was different,' she evaded his eyes.

'What was different about it?' He searched through his jacket pocket, removing a cheroot and lighting it with obvious pleasure. 'The only difference I can see is that this time it would have been me who knew nothing about it.'

'Exactly.' Kate began tidying the bedclothes to hide her

embarrassment. 'I don't happen to be the sort of girl who can get into bed with a man just because it's my bed he happens to be asleep in—even if he is unconscious and incapable.'

'Mm, I don't think I was incapable when I arrived here last night. I just wish I could remember more about it.'

'You aren't missing anything by not knowing, you were just more insulting than usual, that's all.'

'And I didn't ask you to marry me?'

'No,' she said firmly.

'Well, that's what I came here for. I'd just downed half a bottle of whisky and had been trying to decide whether to drink the other half or come over here and tell you I'd give in to your demand for a wedding ring. The fresh air on top of the whisky must have put the thought of marriage right out of my head.'

'Is that all marriage means to you, a demand for a wedding ring?'

'With you it does.' His look was grim. 'You seem to find a gold band the main attraction, and as I have to have you, no matter what the price, that's what I shall give you. Besides a large settlement at the end of the marriage, no doubt,' he added cynically.

'You aren't expecting it to last.' His idea of marriage cut into her like a knife. If she had ever, in her girlhood dreams, thought of a proposal from this man it had never been like this, a wedding ring the price to be paid for her body.

'Are you?' His eyes were narrowed. 'In this day and age, with fifty per cent of marriages ending in divorce, I don't think a marriage based on lust and greed has a chance in hell of surviving. But it might be fun for a few weeks, maybe months.'

'What happened to this once-in-a-lifetime love of the Savage men?' she scoffed.

He shrugged. 'It must have passed me by. So, when do you want to get married?'

'You haven't asked me yet.'

Damien frowned darkly. 'Do I need to?'

'Oh, I think so. It's the usual practice, isn't it?'

'Maybe, but I wouldn't say anything about this is usual. Oh, okay, if that's what you want! Will you marry me?'

Kate felt sure it wasn't the most gracious of proposals ever made, but nevertheless it *was* a proposal, and from the man she loved. But he didn't love her and he made no pretence that he did! He wanted her body enough to marry her to get it.

Maybe love would grow. It had happened before. Maybe through the closer relationship they would share through marriage Damien would learn to love her. She knew she ought to say no to his proposal, that it really was the right answer to make, and yet she wanted so much to say yes to him.

She loved him, surely she deserved the chance to make him fall in love with her. Surely she had that right. And if it didn't work out at least she would have tried.

'Do you—do you care for me at all?' she asked tentatively.

His look was bitter. 'You surely don't expect a declaration of love out of me as well as a proposal! Haven't I subjugated myself enough for one day?'

'So you don't care for me?' Her shoulders slumped.

'I want you, isn't that enough?'

'I suppose it will have to be.' Kate had known from the first what her answer would be. She could do no other than marry the man she loved, no matter how it turned out.

'Do I take it your answer is yes?'

'You do.'

'Right. Well, if you'll show me where the bathroom is I'll have a wash and freshen myself up.'

She hoped her disappointment at his businesslike manner didn't show. She had expected him to at least kiss her, to show in some way that he approved of the most vital decision she had ever made in her life. But he said nothing, did nothing, smoking the last of his cheroot and looking broodingly handsome as he waited for her directions.

She picked up his shirt and threw it at him. 'Here, put this on. I don't want you wandering about half-naked with Josie about.'

He gave a throaty chuckle at her anger. 'I'll tame that temper of yours once I've made you mine,' he promised.

'I wouldn't count on it,' she returned.

'Oh, but I am. I'm looking forward to it, in fact. Now, the bathroom?'

Kate moodily showed him the way, handing him a clean towel. 'You can use my ladyshave if you like. The electricity socket is next to the cabinet.'

'Thanks.' He bent to kiss her softly on the tip of her nose. 'Now unless you want your flatmate to come in here and find us showering together I suggest you leave the bathroom.'

She hurried away, angry that he could still unnerve her with his mockery. She had just agreed to marry him and yet she hardly knew him. Would her love be enough, or would it be used as a weapon against her once he discovered its existence? She had the idea that Damien would use her love if he ever knew of it.

But there was no reason why he should know, not unless he looked as if he might be beginning to care for her in return. She was going to marry Damien Savage! It was unbelievable. But it wasn't going to be easy. Damien could be a hard, cruel man, and he had the power to hurt her so easily.

But she had to take that risk. Damien could give her hell on earth, but he could also give her heaven. And she loved him enough to take that chance. He couldn't really regard marriage as lightly as he had tried to make out, he just couldn't. But he hadn't kissed her this morning—a light caress on the tip of her nose could hardly be classed as such.

Surely he didn't intend for this marriage to just exist in bed and ignore her existence the rest of the time. She couldn't take the humiliation of such an arrangement.

She was preparing scrambled eggs and toast when Josie came into the kitchen, fully dressed in a pair of blue denims and a flower-print smock-top. The table was laid for the three of them and Josie helpfully got out fresh coffee cups.

'I took the precaution of dressing,' she chatted happily. 'I take it Mr Savage is still here?'

'In the bathroom.' How could she tell Josie of her intention to marry Damien after her attitude towards him last night?—Josie would think she was mad. And she had to tell James yet!

James! He would be furious! Damien wasn't his idea of a husband for her, especially if he realised Damien's reason for the marriage. He wouldn't approve of that at all.

And there would be problems about the wedding too. If James would agree she wanted him to be the one to give her away. But what would Damien have to say about that? Plenty, she would imagine.

'No, I'm not,' he remarked from behind them, looking quite respectable again in his white trousers and shirt, the velvet jacket slung across his arm. 'Mm, breakfast. I'm starving!' He smiled at Josie. 'I hope I haven't kept you out of the bathroom.'

Josie blushed under his practised charm. 'No, I'll shower later.'

'Has Kate told you we're going to be married?' He appeared quite unabashed at Kate's sharp look in his direction. 'I believe you have some plans in that direction yourself?'

Josie looked stunned at his words and Kate slammed his laden breakfast plate down in front of him. This wasn't how she had wanted to tell her flatmate of her impending marriage. They hadn't even decided when it was to be yet!

'Yes,' Josie answered faintly. 'I—er—I didn't realise you were—well, that you——'

Damien grinned at her confusion, as he tucked hungrily into his food. 'Kate's just as surprised as you are,' he assured her.

Josie poured them all some coffee, her hands shaking slightly. 'When is the wedding to be?'

'We haven't——'

'Next week.' He continued to eat his breakfast.

'Goodness!' Josie laughed. 'You really believe in rushing a girl off her feet.'

Kate had stiffened angrily at his declaration. 'Now just a minute! I——'

Damien ignored her completely. 'With someone like Kate I'm afraid it's the only way.' At last he looked at her. 'Sit down and eat your breakfast before it gets cold,' he ordered shortly.

Her cheeks flushed with anger. 'I will not! How dare you talk to me like that!'

He stood up. 'All this excitement doesn't seem to have done your temper a lot of good. Thanks for the breakfast. I'll go home and change now and be back for you later. Nice seeing you again, Josie,' he nodded.

Kate caught up with him at the door. 'What do you mean you'll be back for me later? And how dare you say the wedding is to be next week!'

Sighing, he turned to look at her. 'I said it because it happens to be true. Now that we've come to the decision I have no intention of waiting weeks or even months for you. This isn't to be a normal marriage, we both know our reasons. I want you, and you have to have your desire legalised. I'll get a licence and we'll get married next week. I'm not having any arguments about it. As for my calling back for you, well, even if this is a short engagement I'm sure you still want an engagement ring. We'll go out and get one.'

'But—but if we marry now we won't be able to go away on honeymoon,' she said desperately. 'You won't be able to leave in the middle of your film.'

'And I have no intention of waiting until it's finished. Be reasonable, Kate. I have quite a few months' shooting left on the film. And I want you *now*, not in a few months' time.'

Tears filled her eyes. 'Does that mean that if we waited until the film was finished you wouldn't want to marry me at all? Is that what you're saying?'

'You're asking me some damn silly questions this morning! We met—oh, about five months ago now, and I've wanted you since the first moment I saw you. That feeling hasn't lessened at all, in fact it's got more intense. I doubt it will fade in a couple of months. But I also doubt my ability to wait that long,' he told her bluntly. 'So you have your choice, you either marry me next week or I'll take you without the marriage.'

She knew he meant what he said and she also knew from experience that she couldn't fight him, either verbally or physically, and win.

'There's just one thing, Damien.' She licked her lips nervously, knowing he wasn't going to like what she said next.

His eyes narrowed as if he sensed her reluctance. 'What is it?'

'I want James to give me away.'

She watched as his face darkened with angry suspicion. 'Is that to be his punishment for marrying Sheri instead of you?' he snapped harshly. 'To publicly have to give you to another man?'

'I want him to give me away,' she repeated stubbornly.

'And I don't,' he returned equally forcefully. 'We may only be marrying for one reason, but I'm not having it made any more of a mockery than it already is. Everyone knows you once lived with James, just think of the gossip if he gives you away at our wedding.' He shook his head. 'It's just not on.'

Kate stood firm. 'That's the way it has to be.'

'I said no, Kate.'

'Then I won't marry you,' she choked.

He wrenched the door open with suppressed violence. 'Damn you to hell!' He slammed the door with such force she felt as if the whole room shook.

Josie came hurrying out of the kitchen to see what was wrong. 'What happened?' She frowned her puzzlement.

Kate looked at her with tear-filled eyes. 'That must be the shortest engagement in history.'

'You mean he—you've argued already?'

She gave a wan smile. 'That's exactly what I mean.'

'And the engagement is off?' Josie was obviously having trouble keeping up with events, but then so was Kate.

Kate shrugged now, more confused and hurt than she cared to admit. 'He didn't say. He just left.'

Josie gave her an encouraging smile. 'He'll be back. He can't have changed his mind about marrying you so soon after asking you. Being engaged is always a difficult time, it's a great strain on both people involved.'

'But not half an hour after you become engaged! Oh, I don't know why I let him get under my skin all the time. We've always argued. It was silly to think that my agreeing to marry him would change that.'

'He'll be back,' Josie said with certainty. 'You'll see.'

Kate wished she could feel so confident. She showered and changed in case Damien did still come back, but he still hadn't returned by the time Josie went out with Paul in the afternoon. When a visitor finally did turn up it wasn't Damien.

'James!' she couldn't hide her disappointment.

'Charming,' he grimaced. 'Thank goodness not everyone reacts the same way when they see me. What have I done?'

'Nothing. I just thought—— Oh, never mind. Come in,'

she opened the door further, leading the way to the lounge. 'Why are you in London today?'

'To see Damien.'

'Damien?' she repeated sharply.

'Yes—Damien.' James looked at her closely. 'He called us all together for a meeting this morning.'

'You've seen him today?'

He sighed impatiently. 'I've just said so. What's the matter with you this afternoon, Kate? And who did you hope I was when I arrived?'

He was altogether too perceptive! 'No one in particular,' she lied.

'Mm, I'll let that one pass for the moment. I have something much more interesting to tell you. Damien dropped a bombshell on us all this morning. Just as an afterthought to the meeting he invited us all to his wedding.'

Kate felt her heart leap. 'He did?' Excitement entered her voice.

'Yes. It was a great shock, I can tell you.'

'Did he—did he say who he was marrying?' She didn't think he could have done, not from James' attitude. But he had told everyone working on the film that he was getting married since he had left her earlier, which meant he still intended to go through with it. Thank God for that! She had thought her ultimatum had made him change his mind, but it couldn't have done.

'No,' James confirmed her suspicions. 'And I think most of us were too surprised to ask him. Who do you think it could be? I didn't know he'd been seeing anyone in particular, in fact it seemed to be the opposite. He hasn't been seen at any of the parties, hasn't shown an interest in anyone that I can think of. Except you, of course, but——' He looked at her sharply, her flushed face giving her away. 'Kate!' he said angrily. 'Not you? You aren't marrying Damien Savage?'

'I am,' she told him quietly.

'But you can't be! Last night you were at the house together and you never gave the impression that you were in love.'

'He asked me this morning.'

'This morning? But——'

'And I accepted. I love him, James.'

'Then why don't you look happy about it?' He stood up to prowl the room. 'You don't look like a newly engaged girl. I remember that Sheri glowed when I asked her to marry me.'

'She probably felt more sure of you than I do of Damien. We've had one argument already. And it's all your fault.'

'My fault?' He stopped his pacing. 'What did I do?'

'You started this myth about the two of us, made it look like the romance of the century when I lived with you. Damien has completely the wrong impression about all that, and when I said I wanted you to give me away he flatly refused to even consider it.'

'Do you want me to tell him about us?'

She shook her head. Damien thought her to be an experienced woman of the world, he might not want her if he knew she was untouched. After all, he liked his women to know what they were doing, how to please him as they were being pleasured. 'I don't think now is the right time for that. I'll tell him when I'm more sure he'll understand. At the moment it may just make things worse than they are.'

'How can it do that? It's only the truth.'

'Damien may think I tried to make a fool of him.' She knew how his mind twisted things at the moment. 'When we're truly man and wife and I'm more sure of how to tell him will be time enough for that, I think. At the moment the disadvantages far outweigh the advantages.' Damien might not marry her at all if he knew the truth!

'I can't pretend to approve of your marrying him.' James frowned. 'You know my opinion of the man. And I don't think he has it in him to be faithful to any woman. He's a rake, Kate—you must realise that.'

She gave a teasing smile. 'Sheri assures me that reformed rakes make the best husbands.'

Dark colour flooded his cheeks. 'I was never as bad as Damien, never.'

'Maybe not,' she agreed. 'Oh, *please*, James, wish me luck. I think I may need it.'

He looked at her pleadingly. 'Please change your mind about marrying him. I just can't let you ruin your life like this.'

'I love him, James.'

'So I might as well get used to the idea, hmm?'

'Something like that,' she nodded.

'I can't let you——' he broke off as the doorbell rang.

Kate stood up, looking at him as if for understanding. 'That will probably be Damien now. You won't start an argument with him?'

'It's usually the other way round,' he told her dryly.

'Yes, but—— Oh, damn the man!' she swore as the doorbell rang again. 'I'd better let him in before he breaks the door down. Please be nice, James.'

'I'll try.'

Kate hurried to open the door, stepping back as Damien walked in uninvited. 'Are you ready to go out?' he asked abruptly.

Well, she had been, but she wasn't now, not with James in the other room. 'I have a visitor,' she told him.

'Really? And who might that be—as if I need ask?'

She almost had to run to keep up with him as he strode into the lounge. His anger at seeing James could be clearly seen, his green eyes narrowing with dislike. His stance was one of challenge and Kate saw all chance of this being a peaceful meeting vanish out of the window. James wasn't the sort of man to sit back meekly while another man treated him so contemptuously.

'You didn't waste much time, St Just,' Damien rasped curtly. 'How could you be so sure it was Kate I intended marrying?' He looked at her now and she felt herself step back from the distaste in his face. 'Unless of course my loving fiancée called you and told you.'

She shook her head. 'I didn't do that, Damien. James——'

Her brother stood up, feeling at a distinct disadvantage to the other man sitting in the low armchair. 'Kate has just this moment informed me that she is to be your bride,' he answered just as chillingly as Damien. 'And I can't say I approve,' he added infuriatingly.

'Oh, James!' Kate's eyes pleaded with him. 'You promised.'

'Just what did you promise my future wife?' Damien demanded, dangerously soft.

James wasn't intimidated by this man's arrogance. 'I didn't promise her anything, I said I would try. But I'm finding it increasingly difficult to even be civil to you, let alone avoid an argument with you. You're just downright arrogant, and if Kate has any sense at all she'll tell you she's changed her mind about marrying you. I may have to put up with you, I work with you, but Kate has the choice.'

Damien looked down at her, his mouth a thin angry line. 'Kate?'

She knew that James was trying to persuade her to change her mind, but she couldn't do that, not when she loved Damien so much. She put her hand through the crook of Damien's arm, looking at her brother as if for understanding. 'I mean to marry him, James,' she told him huskily.

He sighed, seeing the opportunity for stopping this marriage quietly slipping through his fingers. 'Then I suppose I'll just have to get used to the idea,' he said, admitting defeat.

'Damien?' she prompted.

He gave her an impatient look and seeing her unflinching stare back he too sighed. 'Kate wants you to give her away at the wedding,' he said without enthusiasm. 'Personally, I'd rather you didn't come at all, but she's made it the condition to us getting married.'

'*Personally*, I'd rather not come either. I'm not sure I can stand to watch Kate throw herself away on a swine like you,' James told him bluntly. 'But I have a very good reason for agreeing to it—and when you find out that reason you're going to feel a damned fool.'

'James!' she cried warningly.

'I can manage this without your help,' Damien misunderstood her interruption.

'I'm going now,' James said dejectedly. 'And I stand by what I said, you're throwing yourself away on him, Kate.'

'We can manage without your opinion,' Damien snapped. 'The wedding is next week. I'll let you know at what time and day.'

This stopped James' exit. 'Next week?' he repeated disbelievingly. 'You're getting married *next week*?'

Damien raised a haughty eyebrow. 'Do you have any objections about that too?'

James looked at Kate, slowly shaking his head as he saw the love shining out of her glowing brown eyes. He would make Damien Savage suffer if he ever hurt Kate, make his life hell if he did anything to destroy her love for him. 'I suppose not,' he said finally. 'Take care, Kate. Damien,' he nodded curtly to the other man.

She looked shyly at Damien once her brother had left. 'I wasn't sure you'd come back,' she admitted softly.

He moved away from her, effectively removing her hand from his arm. 'If I ever find you alone with him again I'll beat hell out of him,' he told her threateningly. 'And then I'll start on you.'

'Damien!' She looked shocked. 'I never thought you the sort of man to beat a woman.'

'I'm not.' He gave a cruel smile. 'There are more ways of punishing a woman than beating her.' His eyes slid insolently over her slender body as if to emphasise his point.

Kate blushed as his meaning became clear to her. 'I see.' She bit her lip.

'I hope you do,' he drawled. 'Fidelity will be part of our bargain. Don't get the idea that I'll ever share you with anyone. While you're my wife you'll remain faithful to me, and only me.'

'Yes, Damien.' If he only knew how easy that would be! She had never found any man as attractive as she found him, had never responded to any man as she did to him. She had no doubt that she could be faithful to him for ever, much longer than his interest in her would last.

'I mean it, Kate,' he said harshly. 'I don't ever want to come home and find you with James—or any other man for that matter.'

'You have the advantage of knowing that James will be at work with you when you're not at home.'

'And Matt Strange,' he bit out. 'And what about this Alan you've been seeing lately, have I got to be jealous of him too?'

'Alan and I are finished.'

'You're finished with everyone but me,' he warned her. 'I'm giving you a wedding ring to ensure sole rights to your time and body.'

Kate flinched. 'Do you have to put it like that?'

His look was bitter. 'Right now I can't think of it any other way. You've used my desire for you to blackmail me into marriage. How do you expect me to feel about it—ecstatic?'

'You don't have to marry me,' she pointed out. 'No one is forcing you to.'

'Believe me, I *have* to marry you. This longing for you is driving me insane. I've never before let any woman interfere with my work, but you—well, you enter my head at the most inopportune moments possible. And every time I look at Matt and James I see them touching you. I can't take that any more.'

'And how long are you expecting our marriage to last?' She waited with bated breath for his answer.

He shrugged. 'As long as it takes.'

'For you to tire of me,' she assessed.

'Or until you tire of looking at that gold band that seems to mean so much to you at the moment. Talking of which, hadn't we better go and see about getting you an engagement ring? We may as well get your wedding ring at the same time.'

'I don't want an engagement ring.'

'What you want doesn't come into it. We're going to see my mother later today and she'll expect to see you wearing an engagement ring. So you're having one.'

'Y-your mother?' she queried nervously. 'We're going to see your mother?'

'Haven't I just said so?' he said impatiently.

'But I—— We—— Does she live in England?'

He gave that mocking smile of his. 'Well, we're not flying over to the States to see her, if that's what you mean.'

'But I—I had no idea. I naturally assumed——'

'My mother is English,' he supplied. 'She came back to England when my father died five years ago. She now lives in a particularly beautiful part of Hampshire. I called her earlier and told her we'd be over this evening.'

'Was she surprised? About the wedding, I mean.'

'My mother tries never to be surprised by anything I do. Otherwise she would be old before her time.'

'I can imagine.'

He gave a slight smile. 'Do you have any family we should go and see?'

The only family Kate had was already going to be at the wedding, but he didn't know that. Dear James, it was all very worrying for him. But she was determined to make this marriage work, determined to make Damien love her as she already loved him. Once they were married and she was more sure of him she would tell him the circumstances behind James being her brother. And he would understand. He would have to!

'No,' she answered finally. 'I don't have any family who would be in the least interested in my getting married.'

CHAPTER TEN

'You look lovely, Kate.' Sarah Savage kissed her warmly on the cheek. 'Much too young and beautiful to be married to this disreputable son of mine!'

Damien glanced at Kate as she stood beside him. 'It's a little late to be warning her against marrying me.' He held her firmly against his side. 'Married an hour or a lifetime, she's mine now.'

Kate laughed nervously at the possessiveness in his voice, attempting to lighten his mood. 'Are all the Savage men this possessive?'

'All of them.' Sarah squeezed her hand reassuringly. 'The reception is going very well. If you want to sneak off now I'm sure I can say all your goodbyes for you.'

'An excellent idea,' her son agreed readily.

Kate looked down ruefully at her wedding gown. 'Can I change first? I don't really want to leave looking like this.'

They hadn't invited nearly as many people to their wedding as Sheri and James had, nevertheless a lot of people seemed to have turned up, most of them uninvited. The only guests really invited by Kate had been Josie and Paul, and Sheri and James. She had arrived at the register office with her brother and Sheri, mainly at James' insistence that this was the proper thing to do.

Today was actually her wedding day! It had been a strange dreamlike day so far, and it was far from over. Tonight she was to become Damien's wife in the fullest sense of the word, and the thought of that was quite frightening to her.

The reason for this was that there hadn't been too much

affection shown towards her during the week of their engagement. At first she had put this down the the fact that
they were so busy arranging the wedding, but now she
wasn't so sure. Damien had been even cooler towards her
today, making her all the more nervous of tonight.

'Go right ahead,' he told her. 'You can use the room put
aside for you on the first floor.'

'Excuse me,' she smiled shyly at her brand new mother-
in-law. 'I won't be long, Damien.' She looked at him almost pleadingly, longing for a softening towards her in
those harsh features, and finding none, 'Damien?'

'I'll be waiting for you down here,' he said impatiently.

She looked hurriedly away from the remoteness of his
face. This wasn't her idea of how a bridegroom should behave, and she wondered just what she had let herself in for.
She supposed she should have realised just how autocratic
he was going to be when he had cancelled her college course
without even asking her. When challenged about it he had
calmly informed her he had no intention of letting his wife
work.

But now even his desire for her seemed to have lessened.
When he had expressed such longings for her she had at
least thought there was a chance for them, but his attitude
now gave her little hope. He didn't even show casual
interest in her any more.

The small case with her change of clothing was waiting
for her in the hotel room. They were only going
back to Damien's apartment. He had to be back on the set
on Monday morning, which didn't allow for them to go
away on a honeymoon.

'All right, Kate?' Sheri came into the room after a brief
knock.

A smile quivered and died on her lips. 'How do you think
the wedding went?'

'It was lovely. James had been more nervous about this
than he was over ours.' She looked at her young sister-in-

law closely. 'Are you sure you've done the right thing by marrying Damien?'

'Hey!' Kate gave her a reproachful look, her eyes teasing. 'You're supposed to be on my side. I thought you approved of my seeing him.'

Sheri nodded, taking the wedding gown as Kate stepped out of it and putting it in the soft tissue paper to pack it away in the box provided. 'I thought it a good idea for you to go out with him, yes. But marriage! That's completely different. To go out with a man like Damien is an experience not to be missed. I went out with him myself a couple of times, and believe me, I can understand you falling for him.'

'But . . . ?'

'But you didn't have to marry him,' Sheri finished bluntly.

Kate shrugged. 'You married James, and as I remember he was just as much of a rake as Damien's ever been.'

Sheri nodded. 'I think he would be the first to admit it. But I also think I'm right in saying he would have preferred you to have an affair with Damien rather than have you marry him.'

'*James* would?'

'He doesn't want you to be hurt, Kate.'

'And you don't think having an affair with Damien would hurt me?' Kate slipped on the black velvet suit and cream blouse.

'But I thought you—— We both thought——'

'No,' Kate answered firmly, 'we haven't.'

'I see.' Sheri bit her lip. 'And you love him very much, don't you?'

'Very much.'

'Then I won't say another word. How do you get on with Damien's mother?' she added. 'She seems very nice.'

For the first time that day Kate gave what she felt to be a natural smile. She had liked Sarah Savage at their first meeting and that liking had blossomed into real affection, on both sides. This tiny, still very attractive woman was the only person that Damien seemed to listen to and take notice of. In fact on a couple of occasions Kate had witnessed him getting a sharp reprimand from this fiery lady, reprimands he seemed to take notice of too.

'She is,' Kate confirmed without hesitation.

'How does she feel about the marriage?'

'She approves. Wholeheartedly.'

Sheri moved forward to hug her. 'I really hope you'll be happy, Kate. And I know James hopes the same. Forgive him for being slightly reserved, he's just frightened for your happiness.'

Kate turned to close her suitcase, not wanting Sheri to see her own doubts concerning that. 'Damien will be getting impatient.'

'Mm, and you don't want to upset him before your marriage even gets off the ground.'

'That's right,' laughed Kate, fearing that it was already doomed to failure.

Damien was nowhere to be seen when she finally re-appeared and this gave her time to say goodbye to her brother privately.

'Don't ever be scared to tell me if you need me,' he told her warmly.

'I won't.' She hugged him tightly to her. Marriage was such a giant step for anyone to take, but for her it could prove the disaster of her lifetime.

This was all she had time to say to James before Damien suddenly appeared at her side, his light grip on her arm telling her of his presence. 'No need to go back in there,' he nodded towards the reception room. 'Mother will say our goodbyes.'

She couldn't look at him, suddenly feeling extraordinarily shy. 'Should I say goodbye to your mother?'

'I already said it for you. Besides, you'll be seeing her

again in a few days' time.' He turned to look coolly at James. 'I can see you've already said goodbye to everyone that you find important.'

'Yes,' she said dully.

Surprisingly Damien put out his hand for James to shake. 'Thanks for your moral support during the ceremony.'

'It was a pleasure,' James replied gruffly.

'Right,' Damien said brusquely. 'We'll be off, then.'

The drive to the apartment only took ten minutes and yet it seemed much longer, neither of them saying a word throughout the journey. Kate was silent because each passing second her tense nervousness increased, and Damien just seemed to be preoccupied—something else that made her uneasy.

What was he thinking about behind that composed cynical face of his? Why didn't he speak to her, smile even—anything to show he still wanted her. But there was nothing, just a cold politeness that could have been applied to anyone. But she was his wife now, not just anyone, and he had no right to treat her so casually.

Her resentment towards him grew with each passing second, and she had almost reached boiling point by the time they entered his apartment—no, it was *their* apartment now, the home they were to share until they went to America at the end of making this film. If they were still together then!

Damien went straight to the tray of drinks and helped himself to a tumblerful of whisky. 'God,' he sighed, 'I needed that. I never realised before that weddings could be so nerve-racking!'

Kate stood just inside the room, unwilling to go any further. She felt as if she were married to a stranger, as if she had never known Damien at all. 'Especially when the person you've just married spends most of the day ignoring you,' she said resentfully.

He gave her a hard look, wordlessly pouring out another

glass of whisky before coming over to her. He held the glass out towards her. 'Drink this,' he ordered. 'You'll feel better for it.'

She ignored the proffered glass. 'I feel fine now, thank you.'

'Like hell you do. Drink it!'

'No, thank you,' she said obstinately, and walked casually into the room, looking about her with interest. It was exactly as she remembered it, he had made no concessions to having a bride in his apartment. Not even a vase of flowers to brighten the place up.

Shrugging, Damien put the glass down and walked over to her side. He looked down at her. 'Would you like dinner now or would you like to lie down for a while? I'm sure today has been even more tiring for you than it has for me.'

Especially as she had lain awake into the early hours of the morning last night worrying about whether she was doing the right thing by marrying Damien, whether her love would be strong enough to take her through this, her wedding night.

But she could tell by the deepening of Damien's eyes that his suggestion that she might like to lie down owed nothing to thoughtfulness. He did not have sleep in mind for when she got to bed.

'I'd love some dinner,' she perversely ignored the suggestive glint in his eyes. 'I was much too busy to eat anything at the reception and I didn't have time before the wedding. Do you have any food in for the weekend?' This was the one thing she hadn't thought of during her list of pre-wedding arrangements.

'And the rest,' he said derisively. 'My daily woman seemed to be under the impression that we weren't going to see the light of day for weeks. I can imagine how she spent her honeymoon!'

'So do most people.'

He smiled. 'I can't see myself being that infatuated with

your body. I may want you, but not enough to forget the rest of the world for a week or so.'

So he still wanted her! Kate heaved an inward sigh of relief at that, she had begun to doubt even that of late. 'The fact that you intend returning to work on Monday has already more than proved that,' she said icily.

He moved away from her. 'I have a deadline to meet.'

'And that must come first,' she taunted sarcastically.

'I think you're right,' he humoured her. 'Dinner first. Your hunger is making you bitchy.'

'I've always been bitchy.'

'Definitely dinner!'

She followed him into the kitchen. 'What are we going to have?'

He was looking at the contents of the refrigerator. 'Steak and salad all right?'

'Fine. I'll just change and then make it for you.' She turned away uncertainly, not sure which room they would be using or where her clothes had been put.

'I'll get dinner while you change,' he told her. 'I've had the room with the fourposter prepared for us.'

'How romantic,' she taunted. God, she was so nervous, so nervous it was making her shrewish with him. She would have to calm herself down or the whole evening would be a disaster. 'Sorry,' she muttered stiffly.

Damien sighed. 'Go and change, Kate. You know the way.'

'Yes.'

The room was just as she remembered it, except the bed-clothes had been temptingly turned back—the daily woman again, she presumed. It certainly wouldn't have been Damien. The way he was acting they might just as well not have bothered to get married. He was treating her like any other woman he casually spent the night with.

Because of his uncaring attitude she decided to be like-wise, discarding the lovely evening dress she had been going to wear, and donning denims and a thick jumper instead. Back in the kitchen Damien had already placed the food on the table, putting her steak in front of her before sitting down beside her.

Kate ate the steak and helped herself to a little of the salad. Damien certainly wouldn't starve if left to his own devices, he knew how to cook steak to perfection.

She sipped the wine he had provided with the meal. 'Do you think we'll still be married at Christmas?' she asked bluntly.

He quirked an eyebrow. 'Wondering if you can save yourself the price of my present?'

She shrugged. 'I'm just curious.'

He too sipped his wine, then sat back to look at her. 'When is Christmas, five, six weeks away? Mm, I think we can amuse each other for a couple of months at least. Yes, I should think we'll still be together at Christmas.'

'Oh!'

'You sound disappointed.'

'Surprised is more the word.' And heartbroken. Two months—he had given their marriage a life-span of two months!

Damien stood up. 'Let's go into the lounge.'

That was a step nearer the bedroom! 'I—I'll just wash up the dinner things first,' Kate said desperately.

He took a firm hold of her arm. 'Not just now you won't.' He saw her seated in the lounge. 'Do you have anything special you want to do over the Christmas holiday?'

She clung to her glass of wine as if it were a lifeline. She cleared her throat before answering. 'No—er—no, I don't think so.' She didn't have any plans past tonight.

'Good.' He came to sit on the arm of her chair, so close to her she was conscious of nothing else but his thigh so close to her arm.

'Why?'

'I have plans for us.'

'You—you do?'

'Mm.' His hand was gently caressing her nape. 'I thought we could have a belated honeymoon, go away somewhere together for a week or two.'

His hand was causing strange sensations down her spine and she had the feeling her voice wouldn't be quite steady when she spoke. 'Go away?' she squeaked. 'Where?'

He bent his head to place his lips where his hand had so recently been and Kate quivered with pleasure. 'I think . . .' he murmured, 'that our destination will have to be discussed between the two of us. But not right now.' He turned her face towards him. 'Right now I want to make love to you.'

She flinched away from the desire no longer hidden in his eyes. 'I—um—— It's early yet.' She glanced nervously at her watch. 'It's only nine-thirty.'

He stood up, pulling her effortlessly to her feet. 'So we'll have a shower, *then* go to bed.'

'A shower,' she latched thankfully on to the idea. 'What a good idea.'

'Mm,' his eyes never left her face. 'The shower is big enough for two—just.'

'Big enough for . . .' Panic re-entered her face. 'Oh no, I couldn't! I mean it——'

Damien suddenly looked impatient. 'You can drop the act, Kate. You have me well and truly hooked now, so you can stop the virginal bride act.'

She shook her head, her eyes wide with distress. 'I—It isn't an act, Damien. I've never been with a man before. Truly, Damien.'

His eyes snapped with anger and he pulled her ruthlessly after him in the direction of the bedroom. 'Truth!' he echoed curtly. 'You don't know the meaning of the word. But let me tell you here and now I have no intention of acting the nervous bridegroom to your virginal innocence. I've paid a high price for you—my freedom. That's the highest price any man can pay for a woman. You'd better make me feel it was worth it or believe me, you'll be out of here first thing in the morning.'

Kate pulled away from him. 'That's all it is to you, isn't it? A price to be paid for something you want.'

'What else?' he taunted. 'You surely weren't expecting any last-minute declaration of love from me?'

She paled even more at the contempt in his voice. 'Your sort of person doesn't know the meaning of love. I think I should just leave now, it's obvious you don't even like me.'

'Like you!' he spat the words. 'How can you like something that's tormenting hell out of you day and night?' He bent and swung her struggling body up into his arms. 'I'm going to take you to my bed now and this time there will be no escape for you. I'll have made you mine a hundred different ways before morning,' he promised grimly. 'And maybe then you won't want to escape from me.'

He dropped her down on to the bed, moving quickly to be at her side. Kate could sense the brutality in him as she fought against him for all she was worth. Her kicks and struggles were futile against his superior strength, and her final humiliation came when he openly laughed at her.

'I hate you, Damien Savage!' she cried out.

He held her face roughly between his hands, a wild look about his eyes.

'I told you that it wouldn't matter to me if you fought me. You married me knowing what to expect today. And I'm going to see you aren't disappointed.'

He despatched with their clothing with consummate ease and soon their naked bodies were moulded together as if they had always been made to be that way. Kate felt dazed by the emotions clamouring for relief in her inexperienced body, felt as if she were drowning in the pleasure his hair-roughened chest was evoking against her own sensitive skin.

His mouth roamed possessively over her throat and shoulders before his body shifted slightly and she felt his lips playing with her already roused breasts. 'Damien,' she groaned, remembering the last time he had held her so intimately. 'Please be gentle,' she pleaded.

He lifted his head, his green eyes almost black with desire. 'I remembered to shave first this time,' his smile was wolfish. 'I won't give you cause to complain or to run away from me.'

And he didn't, gently coaxing her to such a pitch that she pleaded for his full possession of her fevered body. But still he didn't take her, each kiss more drugging than the last, each caress more pleasurably exciting.

Her eyes wild, her hair in complete disorder, she kissed him back, his flesh firm beneath her lips. 'Now, Damien. *Please*, now!'

He needed no further encouragement, his body heavy and yet curiously light on hers. The pain she had been led to expect came quickly and faded just as fast, the terror built up by girlish chatter grossly exaggerating a woman's first union with a man. Now another emotion was taking over, a feeling of a dam about to burst.

She could feel the tautness of her own body and knew that soon she must find release. When the ultimate of their lovemaking happened she cried out, feeling as if the whole world were revolving on a giddy axis.

'Give in to it, Kate. Give in!' Damien encouraged hotly, his own laboured breathing evidence of his own fulfilment.

She bit softly into his shoulder as a means of stopping this floating feeling, unaware of the pain she was inflicting or the jagged teethmarks that would remain long after they had come back down to earth.

Considering his previous harsh treatment of her Damien had been remarkably gentle with her during their love-making. He had made it everything a girl could wish for on her wedding night.

They lay side by side, her body curved into his, her head resting on his chest. She felt so tired, so sleepy—and so wonderful. Her body tingled with life and she knew that she would never feel the same again. Tonight Damien had made a woman out of her, and she wanted it to happen time and time again.

'Thank you, Damien,' she murmured almost inaudibly, sleep beginning to take over.

The arm about her shoulders moved and she felt his hand smoothing back her silky hair. 'Sleep now, Kate,' he said softly. 'We'll talk in the morning.'

'Talk?' She yawned. 'What about?'

'I think you know, Kate,' he replied deeply.

No, she didn't know at all, but she was just too tired to care about anything at the moment. She felt herself drifting and didn't know any more until a sudden chill about her body told her she was alone in the bed. She sat up in a panic, her eyes frantically searching the gloom of the room for sign of Damien. She saw his shadowy figure moving about at the foot of the bed.

'Damien?' she queried softly. 'What are you doing?'

'I'll be back soon, angel,' he said gruffly. 'Just go back to sleep. I won't be long.'

'But where are you going?' Her distress was obvious in her voice.

He came to her side, bending down to gently kiss her lips. 'I'll be back soon,' he promised. 'Just lie back and rest.' He moved to the door.

'Damien!' she cried, her bottom lip trembling emotionally. 'Don't leave me.'

'Rest, honey.' He closed the door quietly behind him as he left.

The varied emotions of the last week finally took over and she broke into loud sobs, turning her face into the pillow to cry herself out. She didn't know where Damien had gone or why he had left her like this, but she did know that she would be here waiting for him when he returned, as she would always be here for him until he tired of her.

Finally her crying ceased and sleep once again took over. Damien had to come back here, it was his home. Besides, he had promised her.

It was the return of his body warmth that woke her for the second time that night, the feel of being enfolded in strong muscular arms and held firmly against his hair-roughened chest. With a sigh she cuddled against him and drifted back to sleep.

It was daylight when she woke again, still encircled in his arms. Damien slept on, his harsh, often cynical features appearing younger in his relaxed state. Suddenly his green eyes flickered open and she found herself gazing into their sleepy depths.

She blushed at the warmth of his gaze. 'Good morning,' she greeted him shyly.

He watched her intently. 'Is it?'

She gave a nervous laugh. 'Well, I can't speak for the weather, it seems to have been raining all night.'

'But it seems a good morning to you other than that?'

'I—I suppose so.' She was very much aware that under the bedclothes he was as naked as she was.

His eyes never left her flushed face and he smoothed her hair back as she leant above him. 'I've been a bloody fool about you, haven't I?' he murmured softly.

She felt the old panic returning. 'What do you mean?' Surely he couldn't be tired of her after only one night together! She knew she was inexperienced, but she would soon learn. Everyone had to start somewhere.

'When I left here last night I went to see James,' he told her calmly.

Kate recoiled away from him. 'What did you do that for?'

Damien swung his legs out of the bed, standing to don his robe. He tied the belt firmly, his long brown legs protruding from its knee-length. He shook his head. 'You should have told me, Kate, should have made me shut my foul mouth.' He looked thoroughly disgusted with himself, the lines of strain about his mouth and nose deeply etched into his skin.

'James told—he told you?' She swallowed hard.

'He had no choice. I would have knocked it out of him if necessary.'

'But how did you—— Why did you——'

He moved about the room with fierce controlled movements. 'As soon as I'd made love to you I knew there was something wrong with my theory about you. I was your first lover,' he said harshly. 'After you'd lived with James for two years I knew there had to be something you were hiding from me. I knew there could be nothing wrong with his manhood, he and Sheri appear to be happily married.'

'They are.'

'I know that,' he said impatiently. 'When you fell asleep last night I lay here in the dark trying to work out what was going on. None of my answers seemed to be the right one. James seemed to be the key to the whole thing, so I went and asked him.'

Kate watched him from the bed, aware that he was angry, but whether at her or not she couldn't yet tell. 'You could have asked me,' she pointed out.

'I wasn't sure you would give me the answers I wanted. James wasn't too willing at first, apparently he didn't think it was any of my business.'

'I would have told you sooner or later, Damien. But it isn't something one goes around talking about. But I was going to tell you, you're my husband, you have a right to know.'

He nodded his head grimly. 'Yes, I'm your husband. How do you feel about that? Do you want to leave me?'

Her eyes widened. 'Leave you? Why should I want to leave you? The fact that you now know James is my brother doesn't make the slightest difference to our marriage—unless you dislike my illegitimacy?' It was a possibility that had never occurred to her. Some people wouldn't be able to accept such a thing, maybe Damien was one of those people.

'Why should that bother me, you little fool? I thought you might want to leave me because you couldn't bear to live with me any longer, now that you know what a selfish idiot I am.' He closed his eyes as if to shut out some inner pain. 'I'm not even sure I can live with myself any more.'

'I don't understand.'

He looked at her in wonderment. 'No, I don't believe you do. Kate, last night I took your innocence from you. I more or less forced you to marry me, played on the fact that I could arouse you. I've mocked you, scorned you, insulted you at every turn. The fact that you don't hate me, don't *appear* to hate me, comes as something of a shock to me. Do you hate me?'

'You must know I don't,' she answered huskily, unable to look at him.

'And you don't want to leave me?'

She shook her head. 'No.'

He sat down on the bed, gently lifting her chin to look at her. 'You'll stay with me? Let me try to make amends?'

'I won't leave until you tell me to go.'

'That will be never!' He held her to him, his arms wholly possessive. 'I don't deserve a second chance with you, I don't deserve anything from you. But I love you, Kate. I think I must have been half out of my head with love for you to be able to think those things of you. Anyone can see you're sweet, and good, and much too perfect to be married to me.'

'You love *me*?' she squeaked. 'But—but when . . .'

'For ever, I think,' he answered her unfinished question. 'Certainly since the day I came to see James and heard you tell him you loved him. I saw red when I heard you say that to him. I knew then that I wanted to be the one you said that to, the only one. But my stupid damned pride got in the way. I wanted you for my own, but because you're the only woman I've ever loved I wanted to be the first with you, I wanted no other man to have touched you. Every time I thought of James or someone like him possessing your body I resorted to insults. If I hadn't I think I might have hit out at someone. I've been eaten alive with jealousy, ripped to shreds inside until I could hardly stand the pain.'

Her eyes shone. 'The one and only love of the Savage men,' she said softly, unable to believe that she was this to Damien.

'Yes,' he ground out fiercely, his grip on her shoulders quite painful. 'I knew from the first that that's what you were to me. But I couldn't tell you that, the type of person I thought you to be would have taken advantage of that love. I was already suffering the pains of living hell, I don't think I could have stood any more. But I desperately wanted you with me. I even offered to give you a screen test in the hope that I could direct you. Then I got to thinking of all those other men ogling you and I knew it wouldn't work out.'

So that was the reason he had changed his mind. 'James was rather puzzled by the fact that you seemed relieved when I said no, especially as you seemed so certain I could be a success,' she told him.

'You still could be. But I couldn't stand it,' he said grimly.

She soothed away the frown from between his luminous green eyes. 'I wouldn't ever ask you to. Damien . . .' she hesitated. 'You said you believed I might take advantage of the love you have for me, don't you think I might do the same now?'

He shrugged. 'It's a risk I have to take. If you're ever going to grow to love me you have to at least know that I already love you. As a start I suggest we have a trial separation.'

'Damien!' she gasped. 'What are you saying?'

'I'm making the ultimate sacrifice.' He gave a rueful smile. 'I could keep you here, make you infatuated with our lovemaking, but it wouldn't be what I want. I want your love, all of it. We've done things the wrong way round, married before I had a chance to try and win your love. I admit that was mainly my fault, I couldn't be with you more than five minutes without wanting you. But now that I know there's been no one else I think I might manage to last a little longer than that.'

'And if you can't?'

'I have to,' he groaned. 'You'll never know the pain and disillusionment I went through when I thought you were encouraging men like Matt Strange and James. If I know that I'm the only one you're seeing I might be able to get by for a few weeks.'

'I never encouraged Matt Strange, you know. I detest him utterly, I always have.'

'So do I—now. It's been hell working on this movie with him. The friction between us has been electric.'

'So James told me.'

Damien's mouth tightened. 'If I ever catch Matt near you again I'll break his damned neck. I ought to have done it anyway, the way he was pawing you. The trouble was, I thought you were secretly enjoying it. You know, a case of "the lady doth protest too much"!'

'I was protesting because his touch made my skin crawl!'

'At least I can say that I don't do that. Once I realised I loved you I tried to forget you again. I was so sure that no woman would ever hook me, make me nothing but a helpless fool. I've been nothing but a fool since the day I met you, a damned stupid idiot. So will you try? Will you let me take you out, get to know me, try to love me?'

'And if I can't, what happens then?'

'I die a very slow painful death.'

Kate looked at his face for some sign of teasing, but

could find none. He was in deadly earnest. 'And do you think you'll be able to leave me at my door every night?' she persisted.

A look of torment crossed his face. 'I have to do that too. If you'll give me the chance I'm not going to ruin it by my selfish lust. I want you like hell, but I want your love more.'

'Oh, Damien,' she choked, 'you already have it. I would never have married you for any other reason than that I love you.'

His face was deathly white under his tan, his eyes like huge green orbs. 'Do you mean that?' His look was uncertain.

'I mean it. I love you so very much. If you can trust me with your love then I can certainly trust you with mine. That's what loving someone is all about—trust.'

'Oh, honey!' It was a sigh from deep within him. 'You love me? You really love me?'

She put her arms up about his neck, pulling him closer and closer. 'Maybe you'll believe me if I show you how much.'

'Kate . . .' he groaned as her lips met his, feeling himself drawn down and knowing himself lost in her loveliness.

Kate lay against his chest, happy in the aftermath of their lovemaking. She giggled. 'You've been such a brute to me in the past,' she teased.

'Only because I love you so damned much,' Damien growled against her ear.

'If that's how you show your love I would hate to see you annoyed with me!'

His arms tightened about her and he kissed her temple with lingering passion. 'It was your closeness to James that triggered it off. His mother's attitude towards you only seemed to convince me that you were everything I thought you were. I suppose her feelings are understandable in the circumstances.'

Kate nodded. 'What did you believe me to be?'

'A gold-digger after a wedding ring,' he told her bluntly.

She sat up. 'But you married me anyway.'

He pulled her back down on to his chest. 'Of course I did. I can't live without you, Kate. I kept walking away from you only to come back a few weeks later.'

'I could have died this evening when you gave our marriage a two months' life-span,' she shuddered at the memory.

'How do you think I felt? I said that because I didn't want you to feel trapped, but I can assure you that I had every intention of staying married to you for all time.'

'But if you believed me to be a gold-digger?'

'I had to have you anyway. I knew from the first that you weren't indifferent to me, and I believed that a love as strong as mine is for you couldn't go to waste. You had to love me in return. You had to!'

She smoothed away the frown from between his eyes, realising it would take time to make him sure of her love for him. 'I've loved you since you made all those implications to James about our weekend together before you walked out on me.'

'That long?'

She nodded. 'That long. I love you very much, Damien.'

'Forever?'

'And beyond.'

He was pulling her inflexibly towards him, his eyes on her parted lips. 'That's all I ask. I love you,' he murmured before kissing her.

Doctor Nurse Romances

December's
stories of romantic relationships behind the scenes
of modern medical life are:

A ROSE FOR THE SURGEON
by Lisa Cooper

Was it Doctor Rob Delaney, who had once broken
Sister Anna's heart, who had sent her red roses? And
if not, who had?

THE DOCTOR'S CHOICE
by Hilary Wilde

Nurse Claire Butler had been brutally jilted. How
could she trust any other man — let alone the one
who had warned her not to fall in love on the rebound?

Order your copies today from your local paperback retailer.

Masquerade
Historical Romances

Intrigue excitement romance

THE SHADOW QUEEN
by Margaret Hope

It was Kirsty's uncanny — and potentially dangerous —
resemblance to Mary, Queen of Scots, that saved her
from an arranged marriage with Dirk Farr, the gipsy
laird. But had she only exchanged one peril for
another?

ROSAMUND
by Julia Murray

Sir Hugh Eavleigh could not forget Rose, the enchant-
ing waif who had tried to rob him on the King's
Highway. Then he learned that she was really Lady
Rosamund Daviot — his prospective bride!

Look out for these titles in your local paperback shop from
14th December 1979

Choose from this selection of
Mills & Boon FAVOURITES
—ALL HIGHLY RECOMMENDED

ORDER NOW FOR DIRECT DELIVERY

☐ C211
THIS MOMENT IN TIME
Lilian Peake

☐ C212
PETALS DRIFTING
Anne Hampson

☐ C213
THE NIGHT OF THE BULLS
Anne Mather

☐ C214
THREE WEEKS IN EDEN
Anne Weale

☐ C215
HUNTER OF THE EAST
Anne Hampson

☐ C216
TIME OF CURTAINFALL
(Darling Rhadamanthus)
Margery Hilton

☐ C217
BAUHINIA JUNCTION
Margaret Way

☐ C218
DESERT DOCTOR
Violet Winspear

☐ C219
DARK ENEMY
Anne Mather

☐ C220
MY HEART'S A DANCER
Roberta Leigh

☐ C221
SECRET HEIRESS
Eleanor Farnes

☐ C222
THE PAGAN ISLAND
Violet Winspear

☐ C223
JAKE HOWARD'S WIFE
Anne Mather

☐ C224
A GIRL ALONE
Lilian Peake

☐ C225
WHISPERING PALMS
Rosalind Brett

☐ C226
A QUESTION OF MARRIAGE
Rachel Lindsay

ONLY 55p EACH

SIMPLY TICK ☑ YOUR SELECTION(S) ABOVE, THEN JUST COMPLETE AND POST THE ORDER FORM OVERLEAF ▶